THE RELUCTANT VISCOUNTESS

Miss Adrienne Abbott is the despair of her mother. She is breathtakingly beautiful but she is also alarmingly intelligent and, on the eve of her second London season, she shows no inclination to get married.

Then, to Lady Abbott's relief, Viscount Cravensleigh offers for her daughter's hand. Surely London's most eligible rake can't be seriously in love with a *clever* woman—he must have some nefarious motive for his unexpected proposal . . .

Adrienne doesn't really care, as she has fallen deeply in love with the notorious Viscount. Surely her cleverness must be of *some* use in devising methods to make him love her in return?

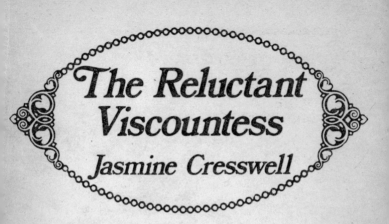

The Reluctant Viscountess

Jasmine Cresswell

MILLS & BOON LIMITED
London · Sydney · Toronto

First published in Great Britain 1981 by
Robert Hale Limited, Clerkenwell House,
Clerkenwell Green, London EC1R 0HT

© Jasmine Cresswell 1981

Australian copyright 1983
Philippine copyright 1983

This edition published 1983 by
Mills & Boon Limited, 15–16 Brook's Mews,
London W1

ISBN 0 263 74345 4

04/0783

Made and printed in Great Britain by
Cox & Wyman Ltd, Reading, Berks.

CHAPTER
ONE

Lady Abbott could not recall the precise occasion on which she first suspected that her younger daughter was destined to be clever. Adrienne had scarcely left the schoolroom, however, before the accumulated suspicions developed into a fully-fledged foreboding.

The final incident, which confirmed all Lady Abbott's worst fears, occurred on Adrienne's seventeenth birthday, when she disgraced herself by discussing politics at the dinner-table. Fortunately, since she was not yet out, the family was dining alone and the scandal failed to become public. Sir George, nevertheless, was outraged. He felt that he had done absolutely nothing to deserve such an odd daughter and he took her into his study to deliver a necessary paternal rebuke. He warned her that she would never marry if she kept on telling everybody what was wrong with the Prime Minister's Austrian policy. She met this dire pronouncement with a most unladylike shrug of the shoulders, coupled with the casual rejoinder that she was not particularly enamoured of the idea of matrimony. Sir George immediately summoned his wife.

Lady Abbott treated the episode with the seriousness it deserved. She knew, even if her daughter did not, that a woman had no career and no future

outside the bonds of marriage. In an effort to get her
problem daughter married off before she could voice
her radical sentiments to the neighbouring gentry,
Lady Abbott decreed that Adrienne was to join her
older sister Lydia in the joys of the London season.

Adrienne at age seventeen was blessed with long
straight brown hair and an unfashionably healthy
complexion. Lydia, on the other hand, possessed a
mass of naturally golden curls and an enchanting
dimple in her left cheek. She never exercised if
exercise could be avoided and so was interestingly
pale. Unlike Adrienne, her allocation of brains was
only moderate and she had never felt any desire to do
something so unbecoming as thinking for herself. With
such qualifications, she was naturally an immediate
success in London society. Sweeping all before her,
basking in the glow of Mama's praise, she snaffled a
baron within her first few weeks in town and was
married amid a great deal of lace and bridesmaids just
before the end of the season.

The best that could be said for Adrienne was that
she avoided becoming a public scandal. This was
chiefly due to Mama's forethought. Lady Abbott
instituted a system of sharp raps on the ankle,
designed to warn her daughter every time she seemed
in danger of voicing a controversial opinion. Since any
opinion expressed by a young girl was likely to strike
Mama as controversial, Adrienne eventually learned
to remain silent.

By such methods, Lady Abbott managed to ensure
that her younger daughter returned to the Grange at
the end of the season with her reputation unsullied by
any rumours of unseemly intelligence. Adrienne
retired to the countryside with relief and spent the last
days of summer nursing a bruised foot and

determining never again to visit London.

There were no suitable young bachelors in the vicinity of Abbott's Grange, and Lady Abbott was forced to fret away the whole of the winter in virtual idleness. She invited as few people as possible to the Grange and strictly forbade Adrienne to discuss anything other than the weather and her new hobby of flower-arranging. Lady Abbott concentrated her energies on pointing out the innumerable advantages of early matrimony. "Just think of Lydia!" she exclaimed at frequent intervals. "How happy she must be in her brand-new mansion!"

"Oh, yes," agreed Adrienne with an innocent smile. "Particularly since her husband hasn't visited her since Michaelmas."

Lady Abbott could think of nothing to say to such provocative remarks so she did not deign to respond. At the first signs of spring, she swept her daughter off to town in preparation for her second season.

For a while, as the grey days of April drizzled into the sunshine of early May, Lady Abbott nurtured hopes of success. Adrienne's cheeks were seen to grow pale and she began to droop with attractive languor. She was heard to utter several remarks that entirely lacked sense, and she spent a great deal of time staring vaguely at nothing in particular. While it could not be said that she suddenly devoted a proper amount of attention to her clothes, being inclined to pronounce one walking-dress remarkably similar to another, she did at least listen while her mother and her maid discussed the latest deliveries from the dressmaker.

"Mark my words," said Lady Abbott contentedly to her husband when he came up to town. "She has developed a *tendresse* for somebody or other."

"Who?" asked Sir George.

"Who?" Lady Abbott repeated the question before lapsing into silence. Her relief at seeing Adrienne behave just like every other girl had temporarily deprived her of maternal caution. She had quite forgotten to discover the object of her daughter's affections. She was, for once, shocked into absolute honesty with her husband. "Good heavens, George. I haven't the faintest idea who the young man is."

"Better find out, then," said Sir George. Lady Abbott reflected, not for the first time, that her husband had an irritating habit of saying very little but all of it remarkably to the point.

Lady Abbott watched her daughter with extra care after this conversation with Sir George. Her daughter's pallor increased on an almost daily basis. She had lost weight and now seemed slender and willowy, the very picture of the lovesick maiden. Her manner, too, developed several reassuring signs of distraction. For the first time in her life Adrienne refrained from speaking unless conversation was thrust upon her. She listened without blinking to the most arrant nonsense and made no effort to correct other people's errors. Lady Abbott, her heart full of glee, began to compile a mental register of eligible young men who might be causing this delicious change in Adrienne's personality.

The happy conviction that Adrienne's future was as good as settled persisted until the night of the Countess of Laydon's musical soirée. Lady Abbott, who found music fraying to her delicate nerves, was seated as far away as possible from the small orchestra and the large soprano. Adrienne stayed dutifully close to her Mama, but by a cruel twist of fate, the chair on her other side was taken by Lord Cross. This elderly gentleman was noted for the stubbornness of his opinions and the complete absence of any information which might tend to lend credence to his rantings. Tonight he was speculating at the top of his powerful lungs as to the fate of the Austrian army at Eylau. Lady Abbott waited with bated breath to hear Adrienne inform him that it had been the Russian army which engaged Napoleon at Eylau and that the French had won. Several eyes were turned upon Lord Cross and it seemed certain that her daughter would disgrace herself publicly by revealing the extent of her unfeminine knowledge.

Adrienne, however, smiled at Lord Cross with vague amiability and said nothing more combative than "Quite so," a statement that was not only innocuous, but also irrelevant. Lord Cross took this as endorsement of his own views and proceeded to enlighten Adrienne, above the trills of the soprano, as to the size and importance of the Spanish empire in Brazil. Lady Abbott was relieved to see that her daughter's eyes never once lost their vague focus on the middle distance.

After five minutes or so, Lady Abbott's satisfaction turned to anxiety. Who could possibly be keeping Adrienne in such a state of infatuation? There were, of course, some notable members of society present, including Lord Byron, who had entertained the company by reading copious extracts from his volume of poetry entitled *Hours of Idleness*. Lady Abbott, who was not addicted to heroic couplets, thought *Hours of Excruciating Boredom* might have been a more appropriate title. For a moment she wondered if Adrienne could possibly have fallen in love with Lord Byron, but she dismissed the thought. Her daughter had barely restrained her fidgets during the hour of poetry-reading.

In addition to such social luminaries, there were the usual number of elegant young sprigs present at the soirée. Try as she might, Lady Abbott couldn't recall a single one of them who had spent more than a few minutes alone in Adrienne's company. She scanned the Countess of Laydon's drawing-room for a second time and, by dint of screwing up her eyes and staring into the middle distance just as her daughter was doing, brought into focus the handsome, saturnine features of Viscount Cravensleigh.

She drew in a sharp breath and sat up straighter in her chair. For the first time she allowed herself to dwell on the awful possibility that Adrienne might have fallen in love, not with an Eligible Young Sprig, but with an Ineligible Rake. Trust Adrienne, thought Lady Abbott wearily.

It would have been hard to imagine any man less suitable as an object for girlish affections. Lady Abbott thought there could not be anyone in London who bore a more rakish reputation than Viscount Cravensleigh and yet still enjoyed entrance to all of the exclusive drawing-rooms. Heir to one of the richest estates in England, he had gambled away most of his share of the family fortune. It was even rumoured that he had recently been forced to mortgage Cravensleigh in order to pay off an enormous debt of honour to one of his gambling cronies. Worst of all, his reputation with women could scarcely be mentioned in the presence of innocent young girls, for he appeared to break female hearts with as much flair and frequency as he lost money at cards. Tonight he was accompanied by the Comtesse de la Ronde, a French *émigrée* widely reported to be his current mistress.

And this was the man who was sending Adrienne

into a state of decline! Lady Abbott shuddered, and
pondered briefly on the tribulations of being a mother.
Since she was not of a philosophical bent, however,
her thoughts turned swiftly to the more practical
problem of what was to be done, now that Adrienne
had shown herself incapable of selecting her own
husband. The soprano had only just finished her very
long solo when Lady Abbott reached her decision.
Adrienne must be married to somebody respectable
before the end of the season, and taken away into the
country out of reach of temptation. She cast one final,
queasy glance at Lord Cravensleigh's devastatingly
attractive profile and sighed briefly because there was
no hope of enticing him into matrimony. Ever
practical, she made use of the soprano's encore to
review her list of eligible bachelors.

Her previous innocent enjoyment of the season was
entirely at an end after this fateful night. Each day
became a grim struggle to see that her daughter was
never in the company of Viscount Cravensleigh, while
still accepting all the invitations that would bring her
into the orbit of the eligible bachelors.

Adrienne herself quite unwittingly aided Lady
Abbott's efforts to bring the eligible men up to scratch.
She was fast becoming established as one of the
season's beauties. Secret passion had improved her
looks almost out of recognition, and even Sir George
was moved to remark that his daughter was turning
out better-looking than he'd hoped for. Dreamy
inattention succeeded in captivating hearts where
intelligence and enthusiasm had seemed merely
gauche. Adrienne's dark violet eyes no longer sparkled
with merriment, but were clouded with the mist of
daydreams. The gentlemen of her acquaintance
listened with eager attention to her every soft and

inconsequential utterance. The young ladies envied her
sublime indifference to the trivia of everyday life.

Before June was out no less than four young men of
impeccable lineage had presented themselves on Sir
George's study doorstep and requested the hand of his
younger daughter. Adrienne, chaperoned by an eager
Mama, listened to their proposals with a modest blush
staining the alabaster perfection of her cheeks. Smiling
sweetly, she turned them all down. Mama, with the
greatest difficulty, refrained from telling her daughter
exactly what she thought of her.

Before the fifth – and last – of the Eligibles could
present himself to Sir George, Lady Abbott decided
that the moment of confrontation had arrived.
Grasping her courage as firmly as she could, she
entered her daughter's bedroom. She discovered
Adrienne, surrounded by the muslins and silver
papers of the dressmaker's latest delivery, staring out
of the window.

"It's time we had a little talk," Lady Abbott said
sharply, goaded into irritation by the sight of such
dreamy sentimentality when there were no gentlemen
present to observe it.

Adrienne drew her gaze back from the window with
a start of surprise. "Yes, Mama," she said meekly.

"I have come to talk to you about Viscount
Cravensleigh," Lady Abbott said abruptly, deciding
there was no point in beating around the bush any
longer. "It will not do, you know, Adrienne. You
cannot have him, so he must be forgotten."

For a moment Lady Abbott could have sworn she
saw an expression of real astonishment written on her
daughter's face. Adrienne said nothing for several
seconds. "Viscount Cravensleigh?" she murmured at
last.

Lady Abbott sat down upon the boudoir chair. She

was finding this interview every bit as unpleasant as she had anticipated. "I have watched you closely over the past few weeks, Adrienne. It was obvious you had fallen in love with somebody, and now I know it is Viscount Cravensleigh."

"But I am not in love with anybody," Adrienne said. "Certainly not with Viscount Cravensleigh!"

Lady Abbott's heart swelled with pity for her daughter, understanding that she was too proud to admit her hopeless love.

"I saw you gazing at him one evening," she said gently. "It was at the Countess of Laydon's musical soirée, as a matter of fact."

"Oh!" Adrienne said nothing more, but a faint blush crept along the contours of her cheeks. "Actually, I wasn't looking at the Viscount," she said. "I was looking at the Comtesse de la Ronde. I was wondering what it felt like to be somebody's mistress."

Lady Abbott's worst suspicions were confirmed. "You mustn't think of such things!" she shrieked. She managed to moderate her voice. "You understand yourself that Viscount Cravensleigh would never offer you marriage, Adrienne. His reputation alone is enough to convince any respectable young girl that he could never make her happy."

"But we both know that I am only barely respectable," Adrienne sighed.

Lady Abbott saw that the situation was more dangerous than she had feared, but she forbore from a direct reproof of her daughter. "Heaven knows, Adrienne, I have no wish to push you into marriage with some elderly widower who is old enough and dull enough to be your father, not that your dear father is dull, of course. But the time has come for you to marry. It's your duty to yourself and to your family, just as it's every woman's duty. You must resign yourself to contracting some suitable alliance before the end of the season.''

"But that's only three weeks away!" There was a note of despair in Adrienne's voice, but she quickly moderated it and said, "You aren't allowing me much time to choose a lifelong companion.''

Lady Abbott clicked her teeth impatiently. "You have already wasted the best part of two London seasons. You are eighteen years old. Before you know it, you'll be on the shelf. I advise you to concentrate your attentions upon Mr Bagley. He is a charming young man and has a snug little estate in Berkshire. You would be close to your sister, Lydia, which would be pleasant for you both.''

"Yes, Mama.'' Adrienne was silent for a moment, then cleared her throat with evident nervousness. "Would you mind telling me, Mama, which one Mr Bagley is?''

"Which one?''

Adrienne ignored her mother's glacial expression. "Yes,'' she said. "All the young men look alike to me. Which one is Mr Bagley?''

"He is the one who always wears a puce waistcoat,'' said Lady Abbott and then wished she might have chosen some other identifying feature.

"Oh,'' Adrienne said once again and fell silent.

Lady Abbott rose to her feet and began to bustle about the bedroom, picking up scattered gloves and thin silk scarves with a great deal of noise and fuss. "Don't worry, Adrienne,'' she said. "I daresay you will learn to grow fond of your husband, even if it is Mr Bagley.''

This did not seem, upon reflection, to be the happiest of recommendations and when she caught sight of her daughter's face, she hurried on. "After you are married, before long, there will be the children to love and to keep you occupied."

Just for a moment, a spark of the old Adrienne flashed in her daughter's eyes. "If my children turn out like me, they will certainly keep me fully occupied. Whether they will be lovable is an entirely different story."

Lady Abbott patted her daughter's arm. "I knew you would be sensible," she said somewhat obscurely and hurried from the room.

Adrienne got up from her seat by the window and walked slowly across to the dressing-room mirror. She frowned unseeingly at her reflection, trying to bring Viscount Cravensleigh's image into focus. She had told her mother the absolute truth: she wasn't in love with the Viscount; she wasn't in love with any man. Her pallor and listlessness sprang from dislike of the frenetic bustle of London entertainments. Her dreamy inattention had been developed as a weapon to help her survive the endless boredom of polite conversation.

She pulled at a strand of her long straight brown hair which the maid had spent quarter of an hour coaxing into a curl. Because her mother imagined her to be in love with some disreputable viscount, she was to be coerced into matrimony with the unprepossessing Mr Bagley!

She fixed a simpering grin on to her face, held out her skirts and dropped into an exaggerated curtsy. "Mrs Bagley," she said to her reflection, not bothering to mask her disgust. "How do you do, my *dear* Mrs Bagley?"

There was a bottle of expensive French perfume resting on the nearby dressing-table. With more enthusiasm than she had shown for any other activity in recent weeks, Adrienne picked up the crystal bottle and flung it at the simpering reflection in the mirror. "Mrs Bagley!" she repeated and burst into tears.

CHAPTER
TWO

Viscount Cravensleigh stretched one elegantly booted foot towards the empty fireplace and appeared to admire its high polish. He resisted the impulse to tug at the folds of his cravat, which seemed suddenly too tight to be comfortable. His patrician features, already etched with the faint lines of too many late nights and too much brandy, were schooled to impassivity. With forced nonchalance he rested one hand against the ledge of the stone fireplace and willed himself to stand absolutely still. Nothing, he was determined, would induce him to show how little he relished this meeting with his father.

He barely concealed a sigh of relief when the Earl of Ashbourne finally put down the document he had been reading and looked up at his son. Not for the first time the Viscount wished his father's eyes would display a little less penetration. His own gaze fell back to the fire. He was not at all confident he would be able to bluff his way through this confrontation.

The Earl allowed his quizzing-glass to travel down the length of his son's immaculately attired person. "I suppose I must consider myself honoured that you have arrived here in a state of relative sobriety and without some woman hanging on your arm."

"Sir?"

"Your reputation becomes more lurid, Cravensleigh, with the passage of every week. It even penetrates the backwaters of the Kentish countryside. Your behaviour, as I hardly need to inform you, has passed well beyond the bounds of the scandalous."

The Viscount managed to lift his shoulders in a delicate shrug, eloquent of his indifference. "It has never been my wish to cultivate the approval of the dowagers at Almack's, sir."

"Your expectations and wishes are not, at this precise moment, of great interest to me. I warned you six months ago that I would not tolerate any more drunken brawls over women."

The Viscount stiffened. "It is not my habit, sir, to engage in drunken brawls."

"Is it not? And how would you describe that encounter with Lord Braxton last month? I trust you would not term it an affair of honour?"

A faint flush coloured the Viscount's cheeks. "Lord Braxton chose to question my interest in his wife. The duel was thrust upon me, sir."

"And is it now the custom to settle questions of honour inside the ballroom of somebody's town house? There has truly been an extraordinary change in the customs of polite society since I was last an active member of the *ton*."

"I am sorry if my behaviour has offended you, sir. We were both – a little drunk."

"That I can well believe." The Earl's eyes, faintly disdainful, rested once more upon his son before turning back to the sheaf of documents piled on his desk. "Your drunken brawls over women are not, however, the reason I asked you to come here today." He picked up the paper he had been reading and gestured towards it. "*This* is why I have summoned you here."

A muscle twitched in the Viscount's cheek. He gave no other sign of disturbance. "I believe that document concerns a piece of *my* property," he said. He allowed himself to give a slight emphasis to the words, then regretted it immediately.

"*Your* property?" The Earl's eyebrows were raised in angry inquiry. "You still regard it as your property? I had not thought you so far sunk in the pursuit of debauchery that you would no longer remember what is due to your name and to your family. This document, in case you have forgotten, records the details of the mortgage you have taken out on the Cravensleigh estate. That estate is not yours to dispose of, or to mortgage, simply because you have gambled away more money than you can afford to lose. I should not have to point out to you, the heir to my title and to the Ashbourne estate, that you hold the Cravensleigh lands in trust for your son."

"And I beg leave to remind you, sir, that I have no son."

The Earl rose to his feet and for the first time there was a trace of emotion in his voice. "No," he said. "You don't need to remind me that at the age of nine-and-twenty you still have no legitimate heir. Would you be equally willing to reassure Lord Braxton that Lady Julie's latest addition to his nursery is not to be laid at your door?"

The impassivity of the Viscount's expression was once again disturbed by a slight flush. "The ... closeness ... of my relationship to Lady Julie has been exaggerated, sir."

"And your relationship with the Comtesse de la Ronde? Has the closeness of *that* relationship been exaggerated?" The Earl broke off his accusations with a visible effort at control. "Enough. I have said enough. By the grace of God, the city merchant with whom you arranged the mortgage of Cravensleigh had enough sense to bring the papers here and offer them to me for redemption. I have bought back the inheritance you so rashly threw away."

"I have met every interest-payment on the mortgage," said the Viscount tersely. "I wish I could thank you for such interference in my personal affairs."

The Earl's lips whitened in his effort to retain control over his anger. "But we are agreed, are we not, that the Cravensleigh estates are *not* your personal affair? They are a family matter, a trust which was temporarily in your keeping."

There was nothing the Viscount could say in answer to this. After a long moment of silence his father spoke again. "I am less generous than your friend in the City. He was prepared to pay you half the income from Cravensleigh even though he was administering the estate. Now that I hold the mortgage I have given instructions that none of the income is to be paid to you."

The Viscount spoke through clenched teeth, his eyes apparently fixed on some point beyond his father's shoulders.

"The Cravensleigh property is my chief source of income."

"I am well aware of that. It would seem that you have a problem." The Earl paused to allow time for the significance of his words to sink in. "However, in certain circumstances, the estate would be restored to you."

"In which circumstances, sir?"

"You are bored, James, and boredom is dangerous for a man who possesses as much intelligence as you

do. You need responsibilities and a sense of stability."
The Earl drew in a deep breath. He was not as calm as
he wished to appear. "Cravensleigh will be given back
to you on the day of your marriage, provided that you
choose some suitable girl. You have wasted more than
enough time disporting yourself as London's most
infamous rake. The time has now come for you to
persuade some virtuous woman to marry you. It is
your duty to secure the succession and to take more
interest in the development of your lands."

The Viscount's knuckles gleamed white against the
stone of the chimneypiece. "I seem to remember that I
had once chosen an eminently respectable girl to
marry. She was forcibly separated from me by her own
family and by mine. I also seem to remember that she
took her own life not many months after our
separation. Do not talk to me of respectability, sir."

The Earl's face showed its first hint of softness.

"Perhaps we were wrong in what we did. You were
nineteen, James, and she was seventeen, the daughter
of a local curate. Not a very brilliant match for the
future heir to Ashbourne." He turned away to stare
out of his window. "In any case, all that is now ten
years in the past. I am no longer a young man and you
must think of providing some heirs."

"You are in perfect health, sir. I believe we may
count on your presence for several years yet. I have no
wish to marry and, with respect, I must remind you
that I am of age. I am at liberty to go to the devil in
whatever fashion I care to choose."

"Indeed you are. Your journey to the devil may
prove less comfortable, however, now that the funds
from Cravensleigh can no longer support your ride.
Perhaps I should point out that we aren't discussing
the future of some small farm. We are talking about
your responsibilities as the heir to one of the largest

estates in England. However much you mourn for a young girl lost to you more than ten years ago, wild living will not alter the fact that you are still the heir to the Earl of Ashbourne. Marry somebody, James, before your reputation destroys all chance of your making an alliance with a decent family. You have to marry some day. Does it matter very much whether it is this year or next? London is full of pretty women and, God knows why, it seems that you may take your pick of them."

The Viscount gave a brief laugh, singularly lacking in mirth. "That is no compliment to me, sir. For the sake of becoming Countess of Ashbourne one day, most women would be prepared to marry Satan himself."

"I believe you underrate your personal appeal, Cravensleigh."

The Viscount inclined his head in an ironic gesture of thanks. "Modesty has never previously been accounted one of my failings," he said lightly. "Your advice and suggestions have been noted, sir. Do I have your permission to withdraw? I have an appointment with a friend to keep this evening."

The Earl placed the mortgage documents inside the drawer of his desk. He no longer looked directly at his son. "Do you have to leave us so soon? I was hoping … that is to say, your mother was hoping you would wait to dine with us."

"I will certainly pay my respects to my mother and to my sister," said the Viscount. "But I have an appointment in the War Office tomorrow morning, and I don't relish the prospect of a long drive back from here in the dark."

"As you wish." The Earl did not press the point, but there was an unmistakable note of command in his voice when he spoke again. "I look forward to hearing word of your approaching nuptials."

"I trust, sir, that you will not find yourself waiting in vain."

Briefly his father looked up. "So do I, Cravensleigh. For the sake of your financial well-being, so do I."

Denby had been with his master long enough to know when it was a good idea to keep his mouth shut, and one look at the Viscount's tightly set features warned him that this was one of those occasions when it was prudent to remain silent. He watched the Viscount swing himself up into the curricle, pushing the capes of his greatcoat out of the way of the whip.

The Viscount gave his servant no greeting. "Ride in the curricle with me," was all he said when the groom made ready to spring up on to the back perch of the carriage. Denby obeyed without comment, although he knew from past experience that the order boded ill for his peace of mind. The Viscount only bade him sit inside when he planned to drive in a manner likely to throw the groom from his regular perch.

As Denby had feared, the Viscount drove like a man pursued by demons, rounding several corners on one wheel and pushing his team of horses to its limit. A light drizzle had started to fall, turning the roads into greasy-mud causeways, but the Viscount appeared to make no allowance for the dangerous state of the roads. Denby didn't waste his energy in useless remonstrance, but devoted his attention to prayers for an empty road. After twenty miles without mishap he spared time to offer the Lord a brief word of thanks for their survival. A close encounter with a stray dog made him regret this optimistic change in the nature of his prayer.

They reached the Swan and Sugar Loaf, a decent

posting-inn on the main road into London, late in the afternoon. Although dusk was already drawing in, Denby had little hope that their travelling would be over for the day. He was relieved, therefore, when the Viscount flung the reins into his keeping with a curt order to see to the horses. "I'm meeting Mr Travers," he added as he walked away.

Denby watched his master stride across the small yard, ducking his head to enter the low doorway of the inn. He gave a small sigh. The Viscount had too many good qualities to be wasting his life in the way he was at present.

The innkeeper greeted the Viscount with a low bow and a profuse greeting. The Viscount returned a cursory salutation.

"I'd like a room, Simpkin," he said. "And some dinner if you have it."

"Yes, my lord. Certainly, my lord. It will be about an hour before I can serve your lordship's dinner."

The Viscount gestured impatiently. "Send me up a bottle of that burgundy which always seems to find its way through Napoleon's blockade. I dare say it will help me to fill the time before dinner. And some hot water so that I can clean off this mud from the road."

"Yes, my lord." Simpkin bowed low.

The Viscount started up the stairs. "I'm expecting a visitor," he said. He caught sight of Simpkin's expression and gave a short laugh. "A *gentleman* visitor. Show him straight up to my rooms whatever time he arrives. He's journeyed all the way from Dover."

"I'll do that, my lord."

Denby entered his master's rooms twenty minutes later and found the Viscount staring morosely out of the lead-pane window. He helped his master wash and change into clean linen without making any effort to breach the taut silence of the room. The Viscount suffered Denby's efficient ministrations without protest, drinking glass after glass of burgundy with the steady resolution of a man determined to get drunk.

Denby spoke at last. "Will that be all for tonight, my lord?"

The Viscount paused in the act of pouring himself another glass of wine. "Yes, thank you. I'm sorry, Denby. I'm in a foul mood tonight."

The servant allowed himself a small smile. "I have known you in worse, my lord."

The Viscount's answering smile was amazingly sober for somebody who was already broaching his second bottle. "But tonight I'm afraid that I see no way out of the trap that has been set for me, Denby."

The groom walked towards the door without comment, hesitating for a minute on the threshold. He seemed to hover on the brink of some further speech, but he saw the glitter of the Viscount's eyes and bit back whatever comment he had planned to make.

"The servants are arriving with your dinner, my lord," he said formally.

"Thank you. Tell them to set the dishes on the table and then clear out. I'll serve myself."

"Yes, my lord." Denby did as he was bid, ushering the maids out of the room as soon as they had removed the covers from the trays of food. The Viscount, his hand closing round the neck of the bottle of burgundy, changed his mind and put the bottle back down on the table, pulling up a chair. He took a small slice of roasted chicken, added some bread and a spoonful of mushrooms and started to eat. His appetite was clearly lacking.

At the sound of a knock at the door he leaned back in the chair, nursing his half-empty glass of wine.

"Come in," he called. With a twinge of disgust, he noticed that his voice was thickened, slurred by the quantity of burgundy he had consumed.

A young maidservant threw open the door, peeking round the portals as if expecting to see some signs of an orgy, for the Viscount's lurid reputation had been much discussed in the kitchens of the inn. She saw nothing save the figure of the Viscount, slumped in his chair beside the fire. It was a cool, wet night although the calendar announced that the month was already May.

"Your visitor, m'lord," she said with a polite bob. "'Tis the Honourable Mr Travers," she added.

The Viscount looked up, his eyes not quite focused. He glanced briefly at his visitor, a middle-aged man dressed in travelling-clothes of sober cut and sombre colour. "Hello, Arthur," he said. "You're still riding around trying to look like a damned parson, I see. Come 'n have a drink. Decent burgundy, even if there's nothing else amusing about this place."

Mr Travers slipped a silver coin into the maid's hand. "Thank you," he said, looking with disfavour at his friend's slouching figure. "We shan't require anything else this evening."

The maid bobbed yet another curtsy and withdrew, disappointed that she had seen nothing more exciting than a Viscount who might be drunk and a middle-aged gentleman who looked cross as crabs. Rumour had led her to hope for at least a glimpse of a few naked women.

As soon as the door closed, the Viscount stood up. "Come and sit down by the fire, Arthur. You look as though you've had a long and miserable drive."

Mr Travers shrugged his shoulders out of his travelling-coat and sank into the fireside chair with a sigh of relief. "I'm glad to see you can still stand up," he said. "These days that has become something of a rarity."

The Viscount sat down again in an old-fashioned oaken chair. The lines etched on to his face were more pronounced in the flickering firelight than they had been in the grey light of his father's study, but now they seemed symptomatic of weariness as much as of dissipation. "I am relatively sober, if that's what you mean, although at the moment I rather wish that I wasn't. I am toying with the idea of broaching my third bottle."

Arthur Travers concealed a quick flash of sympathy. He spoke brusquely. "You are bored again, James, and determined to alleviate your boredom by proving that you can be twice as foolish as the next man. Don't you think it's time you gave up this aimless womanising? Aren't you tired of proving you can seduce every woman in London?"

The Viscount laughed. "Tut, tut, Arthur! You must not believe every piece of gossip you hear. I don't claim to have seduced all the women in London, you know. Not even all the pretty ones."

Mr Travers refused to be won over by the Viscount's smile.

"God knows, James, that you have a brilliant mind. There is plenty of useful work you could be doing. I'd give my right arm to have you on my own staff. And Castlereagh can't wait to offer you a permanent appointment in his Ministry. That's one of the few intelligent decisions he's made recently."

The Viscount stared into his empty wineglass. "I already help you, Arthur, as much as I can. You know that I take my honorary position as liaison between the Court and the War Minister more seriously than most men in similar positions. I can do no more. I haven't the stomach for diplomacy." He flashed his friend a brief, wry smile. "My moral sense, which you find so blunted in most areas, seems uniquely tender to the lies I perceive all around me in government offices. It is no use pressing me, Arthur. I cannot agree to work whole-heartedly for you, or Canning, or Castlereagh."

Arthur Travers made no further effort to persuade his friend. His voice was more sympathetic when he spoke again. "Did you have a hard time with your father? Is that the cause for this sudden access of increased gloom? I suppose the Earl had heard all about your duel with Lord Braxton."

"You will understand what sort of an afternoon I had, if I tell you that the duel was only a small problem." The Viscount took a deep breath, unable to meet his friend's probing gaze. "My father has discovered that I mortgaged Cravensleigh in order to pay off my gambling debts. He was not ... pleased."

"Good God! How unfortunate that he should find out about Cravensleigh! I wouldn't have liked to stand in your shoes this afternoon!"

"I didn't much enjoy standing in them myself. But you haven't yet heard the worst. My father has bought up the mortgage on Cravensleigh, and he is now withholding my income from the estate as punishment for my sins."

"Lord, James, what a mess! Why *do* you get these wild fits of recklessness?"

The Viscount shrugged. "I find life tedious on the whole, don't you? Gambling and drinking and women help to pass the time."

He saw that Arthur was looking disapproving once again and he cast a mocking glance at his friend. "No, of course you don't understand. But there is even more to tell you. My father considers it is past time for me to marry. With a virtuous woman, and the prospect of a family, he feels there is a faint hope I may yet be reclaimed for the path of respectability!''

"Devil take it, James, this is no joking matter!" He hesitated, then said bluntly, "Did you tell the Earl that your affections were ... already engaged?"

The Viscount's mocking glance rested again on his friend. "You have no need to be so tactful. My affections, as you so delicately phrased it, are not engaged.''

"You don't love the Comtesse de la Ronde? Forgive my curiosity, James, but you have given every appearance of a man ready to count the world well lost for love.''

The Viscount was silent. "I trust that the Comtesse has not derived any similar impressions," he said at last. He tossed off another quick glass of burgundy. "What is the reason for this sudden interest in my mistress, Arthur? Are you hoping to take over as my successor?''

"No such thing, as you very well know.''

The Viscount shrugged. "To be honest with you, Arthur, I consider Marie-Rose a ... diversion ... A stimulating companion in a desert of smirking virgins and unfaithful wives. There is no question of love between us, however.''

Mr Travers put his glass down on the table with an abrupt movement. "Your father is right, James," he said with apparent irrelevance. "You should marry.''

The Viscount gave a small smile. "It is reassuring, Arthur, the way you so invariably come down upon the side of virtue, convention and respectability. I have no idea why we remain friends.''

"Perhaps because I am one of the few people who knows there is another side to your character. But I won't allow you to turn the subject. You are nearly thirty years old and it's time you chose a wife. If you don't love the Comtesse, then why do you spend so much time with her?"

"Come, come, Arthur! I shouldn't have thought I needed to explain these matters to you! The Comtesse is an extremely desirable woman."

"I don't trust her."

The Viscount's eyes were by no means as lazy as his voice. "That, my dear Arthur, is because you don't trust any woman who has sufficient intelligence to conduct a coherent conversation."

"I believe the Comtesse de la Ronde is an agent for the French government."

"You may well be correct," said the Viscount calmly. He seemed quite unperturbed by the news that his mistress was acting as a spy. "The thought has often crossed my mind, since she is far too interested in my work for Lord Canning. But that, my dear Arthur, doesn't alter the fact that she has one of the most exquisite bodies in London. For an incurably frivolous fellow such as myself, you know, it is her body which is important rather than her political convictions."

"We think her political convictions are important too."

"No, no, dear fellow. It is so long since you had a mistress that you have forgotten what they are for. I can assure you, old fellow, that one must never choose one's mistress on the basis of her political beliefs. The consequences in the bedroom would probably be disastrous."

Arthur Travers spoke impatiently. "I have no time

for your fooling just at the moment. In fact, James, the British government needs your help.''

The Viscount raised an eyebrow. ''I had no idea that my duties as liaison officer to His Majesty had become so important.''

''I wasn't referring to your official duties, James, as you very well know. Neither Canning nor Castlereagh cares what King George thinks about anything. It is the Comtesse de la Ronde who is troubling us at the moment. She has too many friends in high places and we believe she is persuading far too many of those friends to talk indiscreetly. We have to find out if she is indeed acting as a spy.''

''That would certainly seem advantageous to the British cause,'' agreed the Viscount. ''Let me guess how I can help. You wish me to pause in a moment of passion and slip in some casual questions. Naturally, I must be subtle. How about if I say, *Marie-Rose, your eyes are like stars and are you spying on behalf of Napoleon?* Yes, yes. I can see that there will be no problem in the world in finding out everything you wish to know.''

''My sense of humour is not working very well where the Comtesse de la Ronde is concerned, James. We believe she has done considerable damage to our war efforts recently. Lord Marsh was one of her lovers just before she started an *affaire* with you, and he was involved in our most secret negotiations with the Spaniards. Far too often Napoleon has known what our Spanish strategy is going to be, and his knowledge of the struggles within the British Cabinet often seems frighteningly accurate.''

''Then tell me more precisely what you wish me to do.''

''Russia has recently sent a secret envoy to confer with our Ministers. The Tsar is planning to break the

Treaty of Tilsit and join us in fighting against Napoleon. We want you to tell the Comtesse about this ... there are good reasons why we would like the French to know that the Russian government is planning an attack. Once you have given the Comtesse this information, I shall simply wait to find out whether she tries to pass it on to somebody in France.''

"I dislike exploiting a personal relationship on behalf of the War Ministry.''

"And I dislike the fact that fifteen thousand British troops are at risk in the Peninsula. I am not asking you to do very much, James.''

The Viscount's mouth twisted into a smile. "Are you about to remind me that it's my duty to serve my country, if I can? Oh, very well! I will pass on your message. This seems to be my day for agreeing to do things that are entirely disagreeable.''

"I believe that French territorial ambition needs to be contained and that you can help to do it. You surely don't relish the thought of England becoming a peripheral estate in Napoleon's personal empire?''

"Indeed not, old chap. But neither can I quite persuade myself that the destiny of England hangs on a few words murmured by me in Marie-Rose's boudoir.''

"Perhaps not, James, but who can tell? Are we not taught that Richard III lost his kingdom for want of a horse?''

"Enough, Arthur, I am convinced. I am overwhelmed by my sense of mission. Next time I enter Marie-Rose's arms I shall remember that the destiny of nations trembles in the balance.''

Arthur Travers changed the subject hastily. "What are you going to do about your father's ultimatum,

James? Is London going to be treated to the sight of its
favourite rakehell searching for a bride?"

"Good God, Arthur, haven't you depressed me
sufficiently for one evening? Now you must remind me
of my miserable financial plight and my father's
wretched plotting."

"I think the Cravensleigh estate is worth the
sacrifice of your bachelor status. Lord knows, the Earl
isn't insisting that you marry the village freak. He is
willing for you to take your pick of this season's
débutantes."

"And what a selection of smirking virgins I shall
have! All competing for the privilege of becoming a
Viscountess and heir to an estate worth twenty
thousand a year. Do you think it is the money or the
title which makes me so attractive? Or is it the
combination of the two?"

Arthur Travers allowed himself his first real smile of
the evening. "You have a few attractions besides
wealth and a title, James, although I'm dashed if I can
understand why all the women fall for your air of
brooding passion. Come! Shall I make you a list of
suitable young women? Heaven knows, *your* circle of
acquaintance doesn't include many virtuous
maidens."

"You appear almost as anxious as my father to see
me married off. I wish I knew why you both consider
matrimony such an infallible pathway to virtue."

"It's a mystery, James, I don't mind admitting. But
a fellow sobers up when he has a wife and family to
consider. He likes to spend time at the family hearth,
you know."

The Viscount, who remembered quite clearly that
Arthur Travers had rarely seen the Honourable Mrs
Travers while she was alive and still had difficulty

remembering the names of his two youngest children, forbore from comment. "Oh, dash it all, Arthur, I suppose you may as well go ahead and make your list."

"That's a sound decision," his friend approved. "With a little luck, you could have the whole matter settled in time to travel to Austria with the Prince Regent's special ambassador. Did you tell your father that Canning wants you to go to Vienna?"

"And cause my father to doubt the sanity of the Foreign Secretary?" The Viscount gave a brief laugh. "I prefer not to meddle with my father's conviction that I am a totally worthless creature, quite past redemption."

The Viscount slumped down in his chair with sudden, intense weariness. "It seems I'm doomed to matrimony. Make your list of virgins, Arthur. And God help the woman who finds herself married to me."

Mr Travers, all his points won, said nothing. He drew a sheaf of documents from his greatcoat. "These are the latest reports from my man in Austria," he said. "This is why I asked you to meet me here. I can't understand the troop movements he has diagrammed, but I think they indicate that Napoleon is becoming suspicious of Russian intentions."

"Well, from what you have told me tonight, he has justification for his suspicions," said the Viscount. He pulled his chair closer to the table and flicked through the pages of military charts. "I'll give Castlereagh my opinion about this information in the morning," he said.

"Beter you than me, old fellow." Mr Travers peered over the Viscount's shoulder. "I can't understand those damned reports when I'm sober. I can't imagine how you interpret them when you're drunk."

The Viscount reached for his burgundy with a cynical smile. "Alcohol helps me to forget that it's people's lives we are playing with when we manipulate these pieces of paper," he said. He sipped the wine, and a sudden frown wrinkled his forehead. "Make sure that the girls you put on your list are from decent families," he said. "And, for God's sake, don't choose anybody too talkative. I couldn't abide a wife who was full of her own opinions."

He obviously felt this covered the subject of the qualifications necessary to his prospective bride, for he fell to studying the reports Mr Travers had just produced. "Deuce take it, Arthur!" he exclaimed. "Do you think Bony has already made plans to move against Russia?"

The two men pored over the finely written sheets, and the subject of the Viscount's bride was forgotten.

CHAPTER
THREE

Marie-Rose Briande, Comtesse de la Ronde by virtue of a brief marriage to the exiled Comte, was a dedicated, though secret, supporter of the Bonapartist cause. She was well paid by the French government for her spying activities in London, but her admiration for Napoleon was such that she would have continued her espionage for nothing. Born to a French family with noble pretensions but no income, her childhood had been filled with the indignities inescapable to the youngest daughter of a family living beyond its means. Her love for the fertile valleys of the Basses-Pyrénées was only equalled by her loathing for the whole class of aristocrats, whose mismanagement of their inheritance had resulted in her need to flee France. Her experiences after she married the dying Comte, and was admitted into the inner circle of exiled French aristocrats, merely served to confirm her suspicion that most men were corruptible and all of them were fools. She rarely, if ever, thought about women.

For the first year after the Comte's death she had set out on a cynical pursuit of personal pleasure, until the dramatic rise of Napoleon Bonaparte convinced her that France's saviour had at last arrived. During the brief European peace of 1802 she established contact with the new Bonapartist government and offered her services to the cause of France. The French government, encircled by enemies eagerly waiting to pounce, immediately perceived that in the Comtesse de la Ronde they had gained a valuable recruit to their forces.

Viscount Cravensleigh was by no means the first English nobleman to be smitten by the Comtesse's charms. Selecting her lovers with care, the Comtesse had managed to elicit more useful information in the bedroom than the most highly trained military agents found on the battlefields. Although past her thirtieth birthday she was still a beautiful woman and a skilful lover. It was invariably she who ended the affairs when her victims could no longer be of use to her. Her own feelings remained untouched, except by scorn for the ease with which a drunken nobleman could be made to yield up his secrets.

Viscount Cravensleigh did not fall into the pattern set by her previous lovers. He drank as heavily as all the rest of them. He gambled too much and was so careless of his inheritance that he seemed constantly in debt. Nevertheless, even at their first meeting, the Comtesse was conscious of hidden strengths that had not been apparent in her earlier quarries.

Her original pursuit of the Viscount had been routine, undertaken simply because he held an honorary position at the War Office which seemed likely to give him access, should he desire it, to papers the French government would like to see. His reputation with women was such that she had never doubted her ability to snare him and to keep him entranced.

From the first night that they spent together all this was changed. Against her better judgment, she found herself looking forward to the time she spent in his company and, on far too many occasions, she allowed

herself to forget the true purpose behind the hours
they spent in her bedroom. When the Viscount made
love to her she rarely remembered that she was
working for the victory of her country and
remembered only that she was a woman. For the first
time in her life the Comtesse was in danger of falling in
love.

She discovered that the Viscount was not an easy
man to persuade into indiscretion. Two or three
bottles of wine neither impaired his skills as a lover,
nor loosened the tight control he kept over his tongue.
With her other lovers the Comtesse extracted
information, leaving her pawns unaware of what she
had done and what she had learned. She never
succeeded in doing this with Viscount Cravensleigh, a
fact which would have worried her more if she had not
already toppled over the brink of detachment and into
love.

After they had been lovers for some weeks she found
that the Viscount was quite willing to discuss his work
as liaison officer between the Court and the War
Ministry. He talked to her about events in France,
vouchsafing his own opinions and listening to hers.
Once or twice Marie-Rose felt a faint twinge of guilt
that his confidences, little as they revealed, were
betrayed by her almost as soon as he left the house.

Guilt was a new experience for her and she didn't
enjoy it. It also clouded her judgment. Several weeks
had passed by before she realised that although the
Viscount seemed to speak freely to her, in actual fact
the solid information which he revealed to her was
almost nil. She remained convinced that this was
coincidence rather than deliberate policy on the
Viscount's part, and managed to deceive herself into
thinking that she continued the liaison from a sense of

duty rather than from an emotional need.

She couldn't pretend it was duty which caused her heart to ache whenever business called the Viscount out of town and she was forced to admit she was lonely when he left London to answer a summons from his father, the Earl of Ashbourne. She chided herself for the pleasure she felt when she heard he was finally back in town. She experienced a flutter of nervousness unlike anything she had felt since she was a young girl, when a footman came upstairs to tell her that Viscount Cravensleigh was downstairs and hoping to see her.

"Send him up," she said curtly, to disguise the rapid beat of her heart. She didn't look at the servant when she spoke. She thought she despised the traditions of the French aristocracy, but she shared their lack of interest in the people who served her. She wouldn't have noticed if the footman bringing the message had grown six inches overnight.

Her heart beat faster at the sound of the Viscount's firm footsteps in the hall outside her bedroom, and she actually blushed with pleasure when he entered the room. He smiled at her as he walked in and seized both of her hands so that he could drop kisses on the tips of each of her fingers. She couldn't resist running her hand down the smoothness of his cheek. "You look as elegant as ever, *mon amour*. The cows of the countryside have not splattered you with their mud."

He nestled down beside her on the chaise-longue, allowing his hands to rest lightly at the nape of her neck. He laughed teasingly. "I took time to go home and change, my dear. However impatient I might feel for a fresh sight of these bewitching shoulders, I didn't think you would welcome me clad in a liberal sprinkling of highway dust."

"And now you are back in London to stay for a

while? No more trips to the country?" She couldn't altogether keep the anxiety from her questions.

He dropped a casual kiss upon her shoulder. "I am not planning to leave town for the next few weeks, but I have some irksome news to give you. My father has indicated that he wishes me to marry, and at once."

She jerked in his embrace, before she managed to bring her emotions back under control. She hated the white-hot pain that twisted her stomach at the thought of the Viscount married to somebody else. "If you loved me," she said against her better judgment, "you would marry me."

He caught her face between his hands and kissed her passionately on her quivering lips. "Marie-Rose, how could you make such a wretched suggestion? You know how boring it would be to find yourself tied to me in marriage. Besides, you are perfectly well aware of the state of my finances. I no longer have any income, except at my father's whim. I could not surround you with the comfort you deserve if I chose to marry you. I must marry the girl of my father's choice, but you know she will have no importance to me. My love is already captured and held *here*." He took her fingers and closed them tightly around an imaginary heart. His other hand reached out to caress her breast.

"What of your love for me, Marie-Rose?" he murmured as his lips touched the swell of her breasts. "I don't feel your heart trembling, as mine does whenever you touch me."

She tried to recapture her feelings of anger and rejection but his fingers trailed points of fire over her body and it was impossible to think. "What is her name, this so boring young English miss you must marry?"

"Her name?" Just for a minute his hands paused in

their conquering passage over her body. "I will tell you before we announce the betrothal. I can't confide in you tonight, for I haven't made a formal offer." His lips ceased to caress the white slope of her shoulders and covered her mouth with sudden passion. "Kiss me, Marie-Rose, and let us waste no more time in talking."

With a soft sigh she sank back against the cushions, only to remember that once again she had asked the Viscount nothing about his duties at the War Office. Reluctantly, she stirred in his embrace. "Can we be together tomorrow, or do you have one of your so boring meetings with Castlereagh?"

He stopped kissing her long enough to carry her across to the bed. "Castlereagh is meeting emissaries sent to England by the Tsar. I believe the Russians are about to break their latest agreements with Napoleon. Tsar Alexander never did approve of the concessions his government was forced to make at Erfurt. We shall soon defeat the renegade corporal who has captured your country, my love. Never fear."

Startled by the importance of the information she had just received the Comtesse was silent. The Viscount reached for the pearl buttons of her robe-de-chambre. "You are right," he breathed. "We should not waste time on the problems of my government. Kiss me, Marie-Rose. Remember that it is more than a week since I last tasted heaven."

The Duchess of Exeter's ball was in full swing before Viscount Cravensleigh put in a belated appearance and struggled through the crowds to greet his hostess. The Duchess had not sent an invitation to the Comtesse de la Ronde, and she greeted the Viscount with a faintly cynical smile. "I didn't expect to

welcome you tonight, Cravensleigh. What devilment
are you planning now? Got some poor new female,
who ought to know better, lined up to ravish?"

"How could you possibly suspect me of such
behaviour, ma'am?" The Viscount's voice was bland,
as if he had no idea what the Duchess was talking
about. "I am merely planning to enjoy myself at your
delightful party."

The cynicism of the Duchess's expression deepened.
"I'm too old to be taken in by your flattery,
Cravensleigh. However, it will amuse me to watch you
tonight and see just what you get up to."

The Viscount bent over her outstretched hand.
"Then, ma'am, I can only hope my humble pursuits
will not fail to amuse you. I shall naturally strive, as a
dutiful guest, to be as entertaining as possible."

The Duchess smiled, her eyes tinged with genuine
regret.

"Ah, Cravensleigh, you are wasted on this modern
generation of simpering females. Go! You have my
permission to do whatever you came here to do. But
pray don't, I beg, decide to hold a duel with Braxton
on my dining-room table. After thirty years of
marriage I have developed the most bourgeois
attachment to the Exeter family china."

The Viscount accepted her warning with a graceful
bow. He made his way immediately to an
inconspicuous corner of the ballroom, acknowledging
the greetings of his acquaintances but taking care not
to become involved in any conversations. Once
wedged in the corner, and partially screened by a
large and exceedingly ugly ornamental fern, he
extracted a piece of paper from his pocket and
attempted to match the names from the list in front of
him with the faces of the young women present at the

ball. Now that he had decided to get married he wanted to get the deed out of the way as quickly as possible.

Miss Cecilia Langhill, he read from the list, daughter of the Third Baron. His eyes scanned the room as well as they were able without calling attention to his incongruous position behind the fern. His gaze finally lighted upon a red-headed girl, partnering a captain of the Hussars with considerably more enthusiasm than grace. He shuddered mentally. He disliked jolly women at any time of the day, but he shrank from the prospect of facing one over the breakfast-table. He had no precise notion of how much intimacy the married state would force upon him, but he felt that he could not rely upon never meeting his wife first thing in the morning. He placed a small, decided cross against Miss Langhill's name.

The Lady Susan Hansworth. Despite a lengthy search of the room, he couldn't spot Lady Susan and so was unable to refresh his memory as to her qualities. He had never, in the past, been much addicted to spending time with girls newly removed from the schoolroom, but he seemed to recall that Lady Susan was pleasant to look at and danced well. It was a pity she wasn't on hand, because he really didn't have time to wait for her to turn up.

Miss Adrienne Abbott, daughter of Sir George Abbott, Bart. He had a vague memory of a willowy girl with brown hair who said even less than most of the virgins on the lookout for a husband. Good God, he thought, Arthur's list isn't proving very promising. He wondered bleakly if even Cravensleigh was worth the sacrifice of his freedom and the permanent union of his future to some woman so unlike himself.

He was interrupted at this point in his gloomy survey by the arrival of Lady Burrows, an enormous dowager of determined aspect and even more determined character.

"Heavens, Cravensleigh, what are you doing lurking behind the bushes?" she enquired in her most penetrating bellow.

He cursed silently and stuffed the incriminating list hastily into his pocket. "Hardly lurking, Lady Burrows," he said with a touch of resignation. "I was trying to find Miss Adrienne Abbott. I believe she is somewhere in this part of the ballroom." He dredged up the first name that he could remember from Arthur's list, and then cursed when he recalled that this was the name of the silent girl with the dreamy expression.

Lady Burrows was never reluctant to come forward with offers of assistance. "Miss Abbott?" she cried happily. "My dear Cravensleigh, she is just this moment walking into the room with her mother and with Mr Bagley. Allow me to take you to her side!"

The Viscount managed to summon up a pale smile. "Thank you, Lady Burrows. You are entirely too generous."

Such subtlety was quite wasted on Lady Burrows. "It's my pleasure, dear boy." She had passed her sixtieth birthday and accounted the Viscount something of a stripling.

He gritted his teeth, but instead of making some graceful excuse to escape he decided to go and meet Miss Abbott. After all, Arthur Traver's list contained only seven names and he didn't have the time or the inclination to be over-fussy. He was more and more anxious to get the whole distasteful business of choosing a bride over and done with. One giggling schoolroom miss was much the same as the next when all was said and done.

"I should be most obliged if you would introduce

me to Miss Abbott," he said, taking the plunge.

Lady Burrows hurried across the room and, with the liberal use of her fan, poked a way through the crowds until she halted in front of a middle-aged woman and a tall, slender girl with shining brown hair and misty violet eyes. A florid-faced young man, whose complexion clashed uncomfortably with his old-fashioned puce satin waistcoat, stood at their side. His hand clutched Miss Abbott's elbow with an air of ownership.

Lady Burrows ignored the young man and gave a loud crow of triumph.

"Lady Abbott!" she called. "Miss Abbott! Here is Viscount Cravensleigh, who has been looking *everywhere* for you." Her stentorian tones penetrated to the far side of the ballroom, and she looked with a distinct absence of goodwill in the direction of the stocky young man. "Cravensleigh, do you know Mr Bagley?"

The Viscount bowed politely. For once in his life he was struck dumb. What on earth was he supposed to say when the Abbotts asked why he had been looking for them? He could hardly say that Arthur Travers had put Miss Abbott's name on a list of potential wives. Lady Burrows, fortunately, did not leave them time to do more than exchange polite greetings.

"Lady Abbott, will you join me in the card-rooms for a game of whist? We can rely on the Viscount to take care of your daughter, isn't that so, Cravensleigh?"

The Viscount bowed, but once again he was interrupted before he could speak. Mr Bagley looked singularly put out. "Miss Abbott has promised these dances to me, I believe." He did not bother to conceal the aggrieved note in his high-pitched voice.

The Viscount, who had no desire whatsoever to be involved in a somewhat comic struggle for Miss Abbott's company, finally found his voice and started to excuse himself from the group. He was halted when his gaze happened to light upon Miss Abbott's face. She cast him a look of such impassioned, silent pleading, that he was startled out of his boredom. His excuses died unuttered upon his lips.

Adrienne turned to Mr Bagley. "I have already told you," she said in a clear, soft voice. "I have no intention of dancing any more tonight. I have … I have twisted my ankle."

The Viscount was intrigued by the blatant untruth of her statement. "Perhaps you would agree to watch the dancing with me during the next set? I should very much enjoy talking to you."

Lady Abbott was not at all pleased at this turn of events. Mr Bagley had confided to her his intention of popping the all-important question this very night but their aim had been frustrated first by Adrienne's obstinate refusal ever to be alone with him and now by the intervention of Viscount Cravensleigh. After all her careful planning it was too much to have her schemes thwarted by the very man who had caused the original turmoil. She scowled towards Lady Burrows.

"We couldn't possibly trouble the Viscount," she said. "If Adrienne doesn't wish to dance, she may stay here with me. And with Mr Bagley, of course." She flashed a beaming smile at Adrienne's prospective suitor, who mopped his wet brow with a purple silk handkerchief before creasing his pudgy waist into a bow.

"It will be a pleasure to find myself seated between two such lovely ladies," he said.

There was no mistaking the naked appeal in Miss

Abbott's eyes, which were turned upon the Viscount. "Was there some special reason why you were looking for me, my lord?" she asked.

"Yes, indeed there was," he replied, thankful that his wits seemed to have returned at last. "The Duchess asked me to find you on her behalf. Perhaps if your ankle is too painful for you to walk alone, you could rest upon my arm? It will be my pleasure to escort you to our hostess."

Lady Burrows didn't give Lady Abbott any further opportunity to protest these arrangements. She disliked Mr Bagley and thought that Adrienne deserved somebody better. Of course, it was too much to hope that Viscount Cravensleigh could ever be brought up to scratch, but at least he would give the girl a chance to enjoy a few minutes away from Mr Bagley's sweaty palms and inane laughter.

"Well," she said in a firm, no-nonsense bellow. "That's all settled. Let's leave the young people together, Lady Abbott, and go and find ourselves a seat in the card-room. Are you coming with us, Mr Bagley?"

She hooked her arm through Lady Abbott's, and proceeded towards the card-room. Her appearance was reminiscent of a sailing schooner at the head of a strong wind. Mr Bagley, whose complexion was now more vivid than his waistcoat, trotted in their wake.

The Viscount concealed a small smile as he offered his arm to Miss Abbott. Her own lips curved in response, but she said nothing. She placed her fingers lightly on his sleeve and followed him meekly across the ballroom.

"Shall we sit here?" the Viscount asked when they reached a satin-striped sofa that was temporarily unoccupied. He stood politely while Adrienne arranged herself on the edge of the seat.

"I'm delighted that your ankle didn't give you too much pain as we walked across the room," he said.

She looked him squarely in the eye and he was surprised to see amusement lurking at the back of her unusually brilliant eyes.

"You know very well that there's nothing wrong with my ankle," she said wryly. "I am grateful to you, my lord, for saving me from a ... from a somewhat difficult situation."

"Would you care to tell me about it?"

"I could not possibly burden you with my trivial problems," she said with a dignity he found curiously touching. "Thank you, my lord, for sparing some of your time to rescue me."

"I am not exactly weighted down by duties just at the moment, Miss Abbott. However, we shall talk of other things if you prefer it. Let me see." He pretended to search for a topic of conversation, while all the time his eyes held hers locked in silent, shared laughter. "It is a very warm night tonight, is it not?" he produced at last.

"Oh, yes," she agreed solemnly. "And such a crush of people."

"The musicians are excellent, are they not?"

"Oh, yes," she said again. "And the refreshments simply delightful."

He reached into his pocket and withdrew a small golden timepiece. "I believe, Miss Abbott, that we have another five-and-twenty minutes to fill before these dances are finished. Are you *sure* you wouldn't like to tell me what is troubling you?"

She was torn by the desire to confide her loathing of Mr Bagley and her dread of marriage to him, but convention made such confidences impossible.

Besides, she was disconcerted by this unexpected encounter with a man whom her mother thought she loved. She deliberately thrust aside her surprising sense of intimacy with a man she scarcely knew. She shook her head.

"No, my lord. It was nothing. Nothing at all."

"Then it is your turn to find us something to talk about. I have quite exhausted my stock of party conversation."

She laughed. "We haven't yet discused the floral arrangements, or any of the gowns. Nor have you passed on the Duchess of Exeter's message – in the unlikely event that there was one."

"There was no message from the Duchess. The flowers are enchanting. The gowns of all the ladies are exquisite. We have three-and-twenty minutes left, Miss Abbott."

"You must now ask me if I have any special accomplishments," Adrienne suggested. "If I paint, you know, we could spend more than twenty minutes discussing the composition of my most recent watercolour."

"I have a better idea," he said. "I shall pay you compliments. A gentleman always needs to keep in practice. Your gown, Miss Abbott, is a perfect foil for the beauty of your eyes. They flash an amethyst fire that has already cast an arrow through my heart."

"That's very good," she said appreciatively. "But please don't pay me any more compliments. It reminds me too much of Mr Bagley."

"Ah!" said the Viscount. "I believe that we have once more arrived at the heart of the matter. Since you don't wish to confide in me, shall I tell you what I have deduced about Mr Bagley? I think he wishes to marry you, but you do not wish to marry him. I see that this is inconvenient for Mr Bagley, but I must confess that I fail to understand why it poses any problems for you."

She stared unseeingly into the ordered crowd of dancers. "That is because you are a man, my lord. You cannot understand what it is like to know that the whole object of your life is simply to marry."

There was a sudden note of bitterness in the Viscount's voice. "Can I not? I understand better than you would imagine possible. However, I still fail to grasp the dimensions of your problem. True, you will have to marry, but we live in an enlightened age and in an enlightened country. This is not France before the Revolution. Nobody in your family is going to force you to marry Mr Bagley when there must be so many other young men willing – even anxious – to marry you."

"I should not be confiding in you in this fashion, my lord, but the truth is that I have already turned down ... well, a number of attractive offers. My parents naturally feel that since this is my second season I cannot go on rejecting every man who offers for me, just because I have taken a dislike to the colour of his waistcoat."

"Poor Mr Bagley ..." The Viscount's voice tailed off into silence. The glimmering of an idea began to take shape at the back of his mind. "Do you have unrealistically high expectations for the married state, Miss Abbott, or did the aspirants for your hand all share Mr Bagley's sad taste in waistcoats?"

She smiled and for a moment she turned on the sofa so that she could look at him more directly. The Viscount was conscious of a sudden, sharp twist of feeling such as he had never previously experienced.

"Oh, no!" she said, still smiling. "They were all

splendid young men. I just nurse this foolish dream that one day I shall find a man whom I love, and who loves me for what I truly am. Then we shall want to live together and share our lives. I don't want to marry reluctantly, just because my father and my fiancé's father have managed to strike a good financial bargain in the lawyer's office. Now I suppose you will tell me that I am a hopeless romantic."

"Indeed not. I am not brave enough to attempt such a reproof. I shall merely *think* that you are a hopeless romantic and trust that you never discover my secret."

She laughed at him, not at all offended, and he felt once more the strange twist of feeling. "Why have we never met before?" he asked abruptly.

"We have, my lord. At least four times."

"How could I have forgotten you?"

"Easily, my lord, or so it seems." Her eyes twinkled with renewed amusement but when she saw his embarrassment she added, "I was with my sister, Lydia, when we met before, and she is accounted the beauty of our family. I have no doubt you remember *her*!" Her expression was teasing, removing all rancour from her remarks.

"I seem to remember that she was married at the end of last season."

"Yes, she was, and I am becoming quite accustomed to having people remember me now the very first time we are introduced. The Prince of Wales actually went so far as to declare me an official Beauty. Royal praise is a novel experience for me, and one which could easily go to my head. Perhaps it's just as well that you came along to remind me of the former, less flattering, state of affairs!"

He saw that the dancing had come to an end, and he spoke quickly, before he could change his mind.

"Miss Abbott, I believe there is a way in which I could help you, and at the same time you could help me solve a problem of my own. Would you allow me to take you for a drive in the Park tomorrow, so that I could tell you what I have in mind?"

A faint trace of colour appeared in her pale cheeks. "Why, thank you, my lord. I enjoy driving in the Park. It reminds me of the country."

He found that he wished he could pursue their conversation, but convention made a longer *tête-à-tête* impossible. "I must escort you back to Lady Abbott," he said. "However, I shall look forward to spending some more time in your company tomorrow afternoon. Shall we say three o'clock?"

There was still a lingering hint of pink on Adrienne's cheeks. "I shall be ready, my lord."

He swung to his feet and offered her his arm with an elegant flourish. He derived a considerable degree of pleasure from walking across the centre of the ballroom, nodding and smiling to all his astonished friends. There was a certain wry satisfaction to be derived from the knowledge that by behaving with perfect propriety, he was setting the gossiping tongues wagging furiously.

He shot a surreptitious glance towards his companion and saw with approval that she didn't flinch under the public scrutiny.

Nevertheless, he deliberately curbed his admiration. He was looking for a woman with qualities of birth, breeding and education that would satisfy his father. He certainly wasn't looking for a woman to fall in love with. He needed a girl who was well-bred and good-looking. Somebody who was unlikely to interfere in the established routines of his life. Wasn't that just what he had found?

CHAPTER
FOUR

Lady Abbott was far from pleased when she learned that Viscount Cravensleigh wished to take her daughter for a drive in the Park on the very day after he had made such a point of seeking her out at the Exeters' ball. However, within a short space of time she had talked herself into an entirely different frame of mind. The Viscount, she declared, must have Serious Intentions. He would never become publicly involved with an innocent young girl unless his motives were entirely honourable. A rake the Viscount certainly was but, Lady Abbott decided, he was not a vile seducer of virtuous young women.

She bustled along to her daughter's bedroom in order to convey the glad news that Adrienne, after all, could drive in the Park with Viscount Cravensleigh.

"You see, my love, I told you it would all come right in the end," Lady Abbott said with unwonted satisfaction. "If you will only follow my advice and desist from thinking for yourself, you may yet manage to marry the man of your dreams."

Adrienne felt so guilty about her mother's misplaced enthusiasm that she almost confessed the truth. It was disconcerting to be going out with a man whom she hardly knew, while her mother thought he was the idol of all her romantic longings. Lady

Abbott, however, allowed her mind to wander off at a pleasant tangent and was so busy evaluating the extent of the Viscount's potential inheritance that Adrienne's courage deserted her at the last moment. After several minutes of listening to her mother's inventory she could not help asking, "Why is the Viscount suddenly so eligible, Mama? It is less than a month since you told me to stop thinking about him."

Lady Abbott was annoyed to realise that her daughter had acquired so little common sense during the last two seasons.

"A month ago I didn't think there was any hope the Viscount would marry you. Now it is perfectly obvious that he is considering making you an honourable offer."

Adrienne didn't bother to dispute this unlikely claim.

"But his character hasn't changed," she persisted. "He is still a rake. And a spendthrift."

Lady Abbott frowned. "A young lady doesn't think of such things. Ladies *never* discuss money, Adrienne. We don't understand financial matters at all. And as for the other matter ... Well, I have no doubt that Viscount Cravensleigh will always treat his wife with the consideration a virtuous woman deserves."

"That's what I'm afraid of," murmured Adrienne. Fortunately, her mother either didn't hear this remark or chose to ignore it. "It's time we went in to breakfast," she said.

Adrienne tried one final protest. "But surely it's wrong for us to judge a man simply as material for turning into a husband? And why does a woman have to feel that she has succeeded in life if her husband is rich, or well-born?"

Lady Abbott's face crumpled into lines of mingled

incomprehension and worry. "Now, Adrienne, I trust you aren't going to ruin this whole marvellous opportunity by forcing one of your clever conversations upon the Viscount! It's a miracle that he hasn't found out that you are always thinking for yourself. I hope he hasn't discovered that I let you attend lessons with your brother's tutor! I've told you a hundred times at least that there's absolutely nothing gentlemen dislike more than a woman who keeps trying to show that she knows something. You may talk about the flowers in the Park and the ball last night and *that's all*. There is nothing so unbecoming as a young girl who has opinions about politics and philosophy and other quite unsuitable subjects."

"Yes, Mama." Adrienne suspected that her choice of conversation would have little effect upon the outcome of the excursion. She knew, as her mother did not, that the Viscount's invitation had been issued with a specific object in mind, and that object certainly couldn't be a discussion of marriage. However, while her mother chattered about the Viscount she forgot about Mr Bagley, so Adrienne was more than happy to eat her way through a substantial breakfast, trying her best to look like a young lady lost in love. She even managed to listen to her mother's instructions on how to behave and what to talk about without a single shrug and Lady Abbott was gratified to observe this sure sign of a new eagerness to please. She knew that, where her daughter was concerned, even flowers and parties were not entirely safe topics. With Adrienne, one could never be sure that even the most innocuous subjects would not suddenly be given a new and disastrous twist.

Lady Abbott repeated each piece of advice four or five times and allowed herself to hope for the best. As

soon as breakfast was finished she told Adrienne that
it was time to look through her wardrobe and decide
what she should wear. There were, after all, only three
more hours before the Viscount was scheduled to
arrive for his appointment.

Adrienne allowed herself to be taken in and out of
five complete sets of clothing before she rebelled. The
prospect of arranging yet another hairstyle, making
yet another search through her collection of gloves and
enduring yet another parade of hats, was intolerable.
Despite disapproving sniffs from the maid and loud
lamentations from mama, she insisted that she was
going to wear the outfit which happened to be the
sixth one pulled out from the wardrobe by the maid.
This, fortunately, was a ravishing creation in blond
silk that emphasised the creamy smoothness of her
complexion and the brilliance of her eyes.

She was aware of the faint stirrings of an unusual
excitement as she went down the stairs to meet the
Viscount. She did not ask herself the cause of that
excitement, but she knew that she experienced an
acute shock of pleasure when she saw the Viscount's
tall, powerful figure outlined in the sunlight streaming
through the drawing-room windows. She was
disappointed when he greeeted her with nothing more
than a formal bow. "Lady Abbott," he said before
turning to Adrienne. "Miss Abbott."

Lady Abbott was far too happy to have Viscount
Cravensleigh under her roof to be put off by any touch
of formality. "My lord," she said cheerfully, extending
her hand. "How delightful that you and dear
Adrienne should have such a delightful day for your
drive."

"Yes, indeed," the Viscount replied. "Delightful."

Adrienne spoke hurriedly. "You will not wish to

keep your horses waiting, my lord. You will not mind if we leave at once, Mama?"

Lady Abbot was only too pleased to prolong the time her daughter could spend alone with Viscount Cravensleigh. She happily bade the couple farewell and stood in the doorway so that she could watch her daughter climb gracefully into the waiting curricle. Two sentimental tears appeared in the corner of her eyes. Dear Adrienne deserved the best. It wasn't her fault that she was clever. It wasn't even too late to hope that she would grow out of it. Like a weak chest, thought Lady Abbott.

The curricle turned the corner, and Lady Abbott walked upstairs to her boudoir. "Countess of Ashbourne," she murmured experimentally, relishing the flow of syllables on her tongue. With a contented sigh she settled down at her desk, prepared to spend an absorbing few hours brooding over the latest fashion plates in *The Lady's Magazine*. She hoped to find something designated as especially suitable for a family wedding.

"We have a pleasant day for our drive, Miss Abbott," said the Viscount. He was conscious of Denby perched on the back of the curricle, and in the cool light of day he was perceiving problems in his brilliant plan that hadn't been apparent in the heated atmosphere of the Duchess of Exeter's ballroom.

"The flowers this summer have been especially splendid," suggested Adrienne. Mama considered the beauties of nature (but not the crudities) one of the few topics a lady could introduce into conversation.

"The lilacs last month were exceptional,"the Viscount agreed, then sighed. It was difficult to invent conversation that might lead tactfully up to his proposition. How did one suggest to a girl whom one hardly knew that she might like to pretend to be betrothed?

"We are approaching the gates of the Park," said Adrienne, in a manner which suggested the Viscount might not share this piece of information. She turned her head away, irked by the foolishness of her comment. Whatever she had expected from this invitation it hadn't been an exchange of platitudes about flowers and the weather.

For one full circle of the main carriageway they were able to put aside the problems of finding something to say to one another, since they were fully occupied in acknowledging the greetings of their friends and acquaintances. As soon as they had completed their first turn, however, the Viscount halted the curricle. "Would you care to walk a short distance with me, Miss Abbott? There are some pretty pathways in this stretch of the Park."

She accepted without demur, realising that he wanted to be rid of the groom. She waited for the Viscount to spring down from the carriage, tossing the reins into the groom's waiting hands. "Bring the curricle back here in half an hour, Denby," he said.

They walked in silence down the path for a little while. When they came to a rustic wooden bench the Viscount gestured to it with a smile.

"This is just like last night, is it not? Once again we have a half-hour to fill with conversation."

"You sound, my lord, as though you imagine it will be a Herculean task."

"Not at all. It is rather that I can't think of any way to ask the question burning on the tip of my tongue without causing you offence, so there is nothing for it but to plunge ahead. Are you still of the same mind as you were last night, Miss Abbott? Do you wish to avoid receiving a proposal of marriage from Mr Bagley?"

She blushed faintly, but answered him honestly. "As I confessed to you last night, my lord, I am eccentric enough to wish to fall in love with the man I marry."

"And I, for my part, have no wish to acquire a wife for no better reason than that I have gambled too often and too recklessly. We are more or less in the same boat, Miss Abbott."

She looked up at him enquiringly. "My lord?"

"In common with the rest of London, you may know that I was recently forced to mortgage the Cravensleigh family seat in order to pay off a pressing debt of honour. My father bought up the mortgages from the City broker and he has told me that I must take a wife if I wish to receive the income from my estates. He will not even agree to sell the mortgages back to me. He is obsessed with the idea of my marriage. For some reason he imagines that the married state will have a sobering effect upon me."

She turned away so that the Viscount couldn't see the effect of his confidences upon her. Her expression was still hidden by the brim of her bonnet when she spoke at last. "Is there some special reason why you don't wish to oblige your father by marrying?"

"No," he said impatiently. "But I don't find it a state that is compatible with my preferred way of life. I find women rather tedious, on the whole."

"And yet the members of my sex seem to find you irresistible."

He laughed shortly. "My potential income, Miss Abbott, makes a desirable lure. And when you consider that my wife will one day be Countess of Ashbourne you have discovered the entire secret of my success."

He could just see the start of a tiny smile at the corner of her mouth. "The *entire* secret, my lord? I don't think false modesty becomes you."

His laugh this time was more natural. "Well, I have learned to cut a neat figure on the dance-floor over the past ten years. I dare say that may help my cause along."

"Surely there is some woman whom you would not mind marrying?"

"No, I can think of nobody. However, I rather hoped that I might persuade you, Miss Abbott, to become betrothed to me."

There was no mistaking the faint gurgle of laughter which escaped from behind the brim of her bonnet. Without thinking, he put out his hand and caught her under the chin, forcing her face round so that he could look at her. All laughter died out of her face and her eyes darkened. He stayed very still, refusing to analyse the surge of emotion that ripped through him. "You found my suggestion amusing, Miss Abbott?" he managed to say at last.

She recovered her composure and moved away from him so that there was once again a conventional distance between them. "It was rude of me to laugh," she said. "I couldn't help thinking that even my Mama, in her wildest flights of optimism, would never have imagined that you wished to see me this afternoon in order to propose." She smiled at him, openly, but with no trace of the brief emotion he had glimpsed earlier. "I am deeply flattered by the honour you have shown me, my lord, but I could not possibly accept your generous offer."

"Very prettily spoken," he replied. "I can see that you have had ample practical experience in rejecting offers. However, Miss Abbott, if you had listened more carefully to what I said, you would have realised that I didn't offer to marry you. I suggested that we might become betrothed."

"You will have to forgive my feeble feminine brain, my lord. I admit that I perceive no distinction."

"A betrothal is merely a promise to marry, Miss Abbott. Either one of us could break it."

A glimmer of understanding began to show on her face. "But a betrothal is a very public promise, my lord. It is almost impossible to break that promise once it is made." She turned away, so that her face was hidden once again. "In my own case ... my parents ... That is to say, if I were betrothed to you, my lord, I should not be allowed to go back on my commitment."

"You needn't be the one to cry off," he said. "I will do it. Nor is there any need for a public announcement. If we tell people within our close family circles that we are betrothed, I am sure it will be sufficient to achieve my aims."

"Your father wishes to see you married. Do you really think that a brief, private engagement, will serve your purpose? Won't he be suspicious?"

"You are an eligible bride, Miss Abbott, with an impeccable reputation. I cannot see why my father should suspect a trick. I hope ... I believe ... that he would restore the Cravensleigh estate to me on the strength of our betrothal. It is certainly worth making the effort."

"I see."

She said nothing more, and the Viscount spoke urgently. "Consider, Miss Abbott, there are advantages for you. If you are betrothed to me, your parents can't expect you to listen to a proposal from Mr Bagley. And by the time we call a halt to the pretence, the season will be at an end and Mr Bagley safely removed from London."

She gave a small laugh. "I must be in truly desperate straits if I am prepared to accept the miserable role of jilted bride in order to avoid accepting Mr Bagley's proposal!"

He seized her hands eagerly. "Does that mean you will accept? You will agree to the pretence?"

She looked down at his lean, strong fingers which still covered her hands. She shivered with an unfamiliar excitement, before wrenching her hands out of his clasp. It was easier to think when she could no longer feel the strength of his hand touching her own. "My lord, I am tempted, but we should not. We can't do such a thing. There would be such a scandal when the betrothal was ended! And it's wrong to deceive our families in such a fashion."

"Is it?" Once again he took her hands and forced her to look at him. "Is it?" he asked again. "Do you think it's right that your parents should coerce you into marriage with a man whom you don't even like? Is it right that my father should buy up my debts and then use them as a lever to force me into a course of action I don't wish to take? Is that fair, Miss Abbott?"

"No," she whispered, and dragged her gaze away from the fierce light of his grey eyes. "That is unfair too." She had to keep her eyes turned away, but even so she felt mesmerised by the power that seemed to flow into her from his touch.

"Will you help me?"

"No!" She gasped out the denial, but once more he placed his hand beneath her chin, forcing her to turn her face up and meet his eyes.

"I am … pleading … with you, Miss Abbott."

"I … No. Oh, very well! I will pretend to be betrothed to you, but privately, and just for a little while."

He did not disguise his exuberance at her reply.

"My dear Miss Abbott," he said. "You have made me the happiest of men."

"I don't doubt it," she said dryly. "I hope you feel equally happy when you have to face my parents with the news that our betrothal is at an end. You had better come equipped with smelling salts for my mother."

He frowned. "You need not trouble yourself about the ending of the betrothal," he said. "You may rest assured that I shall do it in such a way as to leave no blame attached to yourself."

He saw that she was far from convinced and he sprang to his feet before she could think of any more objections to his schemes. He tucked her arm through his own and started to stroll back down the path towards the main carriageway. "I shall seek an interview with your father this evening," he said. "And then I shall post down to Kent tomorrow and tell my father the good news. With any luck, we can begin and end the betrothal within the space of a month. It will be one of the shortest engagements on record, I think!"

He could see that new worries were forming in her mind with every sentence that he uttered and, in order to distract her attention from the flaws of his proposition, he pointed out an opulent gilded carriage that was passing them a little way in the distance.

"It's Mr Rothschild's carriage, isn't it?" she asked, her interest successfully diverted.

"Yes," he said, surprised that she should even recognise the famous banker. "We should all be grateful to him, since he has just arranged financing, virtually single-handed, to pay our troops in the Peninsula."

"Our Ministers are luckier than they deserve,"

Adrienne exclaimed, quite forgetting every one of Mama's Rules for Polite Conversation. "Canning and Castlereagh do nothing except bicker over who is responsible for the latest débâcle in the Peninsula and I sometimes wonder if the Prime Minister knows where the Peninsula really is. The King certainly doesn't!"

He was amused by her ire, which gave her the appearance of a delicate kitten made suddenly angry, and so was oblivious to the many interested glances being cast at them from passing carriages. He even forgot that he disliked ladies who had opinions of their own. "Are you an admirer of our new commander in Portugal?" he asked.

"Sir Arthur Wellesley? He is certainly a clever strategist. But whether he can coerce starving peasants into fighting against twenty thousand veteran French soldiers, trained by Napoleon, is another matter."

"Do not tell me that you are a secret admirer of the French emperor?"

"No, of course not. But only a fool would fail to be impressed by a man who has achieved what Bonaparte has achieved."

"Our government, then, must be composed largely of fools."

She laughed up at him. "Is that any news to either of us?" She bit her lip in vexation when she realised at last just what she had said. She could only be thankful that her mother wasn't near enough to hear her dreadful breaches of feminine propriety. "Of course," she said hastily, "I know nothing about politics or international affairs."

"I can see that," the Viscount said and smiled down at the worried face she turned up towards him.

Lady Burrows drove past them at this precise moment. She gave a satisfied exclamation and turned to her companion in the barouche, who happened to be the Duchess of Exeter. "Ha!" she remarked. "I suspected something was afoot last night. There'll be some interesting news from that quarter before long, I'll wager."

The Duchess raised an incredulous eyebrow. "Cravensleigh and the young Abbott girl? My dear Pamela, you must have been drinking too much champagne with your breakfast. She is a sweet child, but Cravensleigh is no more likely to marry some chit fresh out of the schoolroom than I am."

Lady Burrows merely smiled. "I shall look for a handsome note of apology when you are proven wrong."

The Duchess of Exeter gave a lazy smile. "If I am wrong, Pamela, you shall have it."

Denby finally arrived with the curricle, full of apologies and explanations. One of the horses had cast a shoe, necessitating the immediate services of a farrier. The Viscount and Adrienne avoided each other's eyes as Denby told his tale of woe. Each of them was disconcerted to realise that more than an hour had passed by since Denby left, and neither of them had been aware of the delay.

Their conversation during the drive back was kept to the most neutral of topics. They were both preoccupied with thoughts of their own, and neither noticed how easily they were falling into the habit of answering half-completed questions and comments by the other. Denby, however, was astonished. He was accustomed to listening to his master conduct either an expert seduction or the most strained of polite conversations. This easy interchange of thoughts was outside anything he had previously experienced in all his years with the Viscount.

His surprise was compounded when they arrived back at Miss Abbott's house. The Viscount sprang down from the curricle and, as usual, handed the horses into Denby's keeping.

"I shall come and see Sir George right away," said the Viscount to Adrienne.

"My lord, are you sure? Should we go ahead with this wild scheme?"

"Why not?" said the Viscount casually, while Denby struggled to make head or tail of the obscure conversation.

"Then I suppose I must face up to Mama," said Adrienne with a reluctant sigh.

The Viscount smiled. "You are not going to pretend that she will be unhappy at the outcome of our drive?"

A mischievous grin flickered across Adrienne's face. "Puffing off your consequence, my lord? Never fear. The Earldom of Ashbourne and twenty thousand pounds per annum are enough to satisfy the most exacting of mothers."

Denby regretted the fact that he couldn't hear his master's answer to this interesting exchange. The butler to the Abbott household, unfortunately, opened the front door, and the Viscount and his companion vanished into the recesses of the oak-panelled hall. Regretfully, Denby began to walk the horses.

Lady Abbott sank back against the cushions of her sofa, too overcome by emotion to speak. She finally regained her breath. "*Betrothed*?" she squeaked. "Viscount Cravensleigh asked you to marry him? Oh my dear, *darling*, daughter, how happy you will be!

And how *clever* of you to have fallen in love with him already! So marvellously convenient!''

Adrienne winced at the number of deceptions she was practising upon her mother. She was unprepared for such a display of maternal rapture. "Perhaps Papa will not give his consent," she said hopefully. "After all, the Viscount has a great many debts."

Lady Abbott's happy smiles changed into a sigh of resignation. "It is a total mystery to me, Adrienne, how you can be so clever and so addle-brained all at the same time. Viscount Cravensleigh is temporarily embarrassed for funds, but he is in no way ineligible. His future prospects are simply marvellous. And to think he has offered for *you* after ten years as a hardened bachelor! You will be so happy together! When I saw the fashion-plate for that blue silk dress this afternoon, I knew it was fate." She clasped her hands rapturously to her bosom. "I always knew you were destined for a great marriage! Countess of Ashbourne … how elegant it sounds!"

Adrienne's feelings of guilt increased with every happy exclamation. "We are only betrothed, you know. We aren't married yet."

Lady Abbott was perfectly accustomed to not understanding the point of at least half the remarks her daughter uttered. This, however, was too much to slip past her. "What in the world has that to do with anything? First, you have to be betrothed, then you will be married. It is as inevitable as day following night. How provoking that your sister should be enceinte. Now we either have to go ahead with the nuptial ceremony without her, or else we must wait until she has been confined and can go into society again."

"Oh, that's no problem! We will wait until after she

has the baby," said Adrienne fervently. "There is no need to rush things, you know."

Lady Abbott cast her daughter a keen glance. "If you are worrying about the fulfilment of your wifely duties, Adrienne, I'm sure you will find the Viscount a reasonable man." She coughed several times before proceeding with her speech. "The Viscount has a ... We ..., the Viscount's ... er ... animal appetites are being satisfied by another woman. You will have to give him an heir, of course. But I'm sure he will not make unreasonable demands."

"I had forgotten about the Comtesse de la Ronde," said Adrienne meditatively. "I wonder what she will think of all this?" She saw that her mother was about to embark upon another scandalised dissertation upon the duties of a wife, and she made haste to divert her. "Shall we stay on in town for a while? I dare say it would seem somewhat rude if we left for the Grange just when the Viscount has made his offer." Now that there was no need to fend off the unwelcome attentions of an assortment of hopeful young men she rather liked the prospect of spending some time in London. The fact that she would be remaining close to the Viscount had nothing, of course, to do with her wish to stay in London.

Lady Abbott was diverted from her lecture on marital duty. "I must speak to your father at once," she said happily. She sprang up from her sofa. "Dearest Adrienne, you have given me a new lease on life. I knew you would find somebody in the end who didn't mind that you were clever! What a great deal there is to be done, I'm sure I don't know how I shall get through the half of it." She bustled off, bursting with all the energy of a mother whose schemes have been crowned with success.

Adrienne walked back to her own room considerably more slowly. She stared at herself in the mirror as she pulled off her gloves. She touched her hand to her burning cheeks and tried to ignore the excited sparkle lighting the depths of her eyes.

She whirled away in sudden anger. "Animal appetites!" she muttered. "Who cares about his animal appetites? The Comtesse is welcome to him." She tugged viciously at the bellrope, wondering why it was that her heart contracted with pain at the thought of the Viscount, his dark eyes alight with passion, as he swept the Comtesse into his arms.

CHAPTER
FIVE

Arthur Travers sprang up from the Viscount's most comfortable chair, obviously not soothed by the silken welcome of its padded seat. He paced restlessly about the small sitting-room, his normally placid features wrinkled with anxiety.

"Are you sure, James, that you told the Comtesse about the Russian envoy? Did she understand that the Russians have been meeting secretly with Castlereagh?" he asked for the second time. "I'm pretty well convinced that she will pass the information on to the French government, don't you agree?"

Before the Viscount could answer either of his questions, he had resumed his restless pacing. "We are trying to spread word of these 'secret' meetings by every method we know. We are counting on the French government finding out that the Russians have broken the Treaty of Tilsit. God knows, we need to do something to divert Napoleon's attention from the Peninsula. Our armies are in no shape to stand up to an attack led by Bony himself."

"So you are planning to set up the Russians as a fresh target for Bonaparte's armies?" The Viscount examined his fingertips with studied indifference. "I suppose it's an admirable plan. After all, Russian peasants are eminently expendable."

Arthur Travers jerked his shoulders in self-conscious irritation. "Damn it, James, you know that they are not. However, I am an Englishman and I consider them at least as expendable as British soldiers and sailors. I don't see any reason why we should be left alone to defend the rest of the world against some Corsican corporal who has developed ideas above his station."

"Hardly above his station, Arthur, since he seems perfectly capable of elevating himself to whatever stature his grandiose ideas demand. He has been Emperor for almost five years and it would be a brave fool who suggested that he lacks any of the necessary imperial qualities." The Viscount saw that his friend was on the verge of real anger, and he murmured quietly, "Forgive me, Arthur. I am constantly plagued by these most un-English moments of self-doubt."

Mr Travers spoke with a snap that barely concealed his own discomfort. "England doesn't have time for the luxury of moral questioning just at the moment, James. Wellesley may have established himself as our nation's latest hero, and I hope to God he continues to be the general he has so far proved himself to be. But he is mortal and we can't look for him to perform miracles on a daily basis. At the moment, it seems our government is expecting him to conduct the war single-handed, while the Foreign Secretary and the Secretary for War fight out their personal squabbles."

The Viscount stood up and poured out a glass of brandy, handing it to his friend with a reassuring clap on the shoulder. "Here, Arthur, take heart. Marie-Rose accepted my carefully dropped indiscretion with alacrity. It's deflating to one's self-image, you know, when one's mistress is entirely willing to consider one an over-talkative fool."

Mr Travers gave a brief bark of laughter. "That rankles, does it? Never mind, James. You may console yourself that you acted in the best interests of your country, even if you had to appear a fool in order to do so. Only think how flattering that, despite what she must consider your lack of intelligence, the Comtesse still seeks your company."

The Viscount's voice was cynical. "Skill in the bedroom can compensate for many other failings, I believe."

Mr Travers face fell back into its worried wrinkles. "That reminds me, how did she take the news of your forthcoming marriage? I hope you won't feel any need to sever your relationship with her. There are several other pieces of misinformation the Foreign Secretary would like passed to the French, and this seems an excellent method. I believe you've decided to marry Sir George Abbott's daughter. Good-looking chit, well-bred, sound family, that's why I put her on my list. I daresay she's your best choice. Your father will be pleased."

The Viscount was startled out of his habitual poise, horrified to discover that Arthur already knew about his supposed betrothal. "Good God, Arthur! What makes you think I plan to marry Miss Abbott? I only met the girl a few nights ago, and now you have me ready to wed her! How in heaven's name did you hear that piece of gossip?"

It was Mr Traver's turn to look astonished. "Well, James, old fellow, you spent half an hour talking to her at the Duchess of Exeter's ball, and then you took her driving in the Park the very next day. Half London saw you wandering about one of the most deserted walks without a hint of a chaperone. What were people supposed to think? Everybody wondered why you'd decided to drop the handkerchief at last, and I felt very well pleased with myself, I can tell you, since I thought I had the inside story on the whole business."

The Viscount tossed off the remainder of his brandy in appalled silence. He turned to his friend with an attempt at a smile. "I have been defying the conventions too long, Arthur. I had completely forgotten that two minutes' conversation with a young girl denotes a special degree of interest and that half an hour alone is the equivalent of a formal declaration of devotion."

Mr Travers's voice was dry. "As a widower with four young daughters, allow me to assure you that society has been waiting for the news of a betrothal ever since you completed your first turn of the Park with Miss Abbott." He smiled sympathetically at the Viscount, with all the comfortable condescension of a man who has done his duty in the marriage stakes and has no intention of repeating his errors. "Take the word of a veteran, old fellow. If you have not already proposed, then do so without delay. Bite the bullet and see the parson. She's a splendid-looking gal and she seems a docile enough young woman. Good reputation, doesn't push herself forward. Not one of these dreadful bluestockings. She'll please your mother and your sister, and she'll satisfy your father. You can take care never to see her if you find out later on that you don't suit."

He reflected cheerfully on his own marriage and gave the Viscount another reassuring thump on the shoulder. "Doubt if I saw Fanny more than a month out of the year in the twelve years of our marriage. Six children, too. It's amazing!" He fell momentarily silent, contemplating anew the wonders of his marriage, a highly successful one from his own point of view and, as far as he knew, from Fanny's point of view as well.

The Viscount looked less than comforted by his friend's picture of marital bliss. An unexpected memory caused a smile to flicker briefly at the corners of his mouth. "I don't think Miss Abbott would agree with your portrayal of the joys of matrimony, Arthur." He wondered quickly how much he would have to confide in his friend. It was disturbing to learn that London society was waiting avidly for news of his betrothal. He didn't want Miss Abbott to suffer when their sudden intimacy finished as precipitously as it had begun. "Miss Abbott and I..." he hesitated, then continued more firmly. "Miss Abbott and I are considering a betrothal, Arthur. I am posting down to Ashbourne tomorrow to give my father the news. I hope he gives me my estate back, I don't mind confessing."

Mr Travers gave his friend an enthusiastic handshake. "That's the best news I've heard this month, James! A wife is just what you need. Dashed ridiculous that a man with your talents should fritter them away, gambling until you almost threw away your inheritance."

"I was bored," said the Viscount as if this were a total explanation. Abruptly he swung to his feet. "But you are right about one thing: losing Cravensleigh was the act of a fool, and in that regard at least, I have learned my lesson."

"Seeing the Comtesse tonight?" Mr Travers saw no conflict between the Viscount's announcement of his brand-new betrothal and a plan to visit his mistress.

"Yes, I believe so. I must tell her I shall be out of town for a couple of days."

"Good. Make sure that she knows the Russian

envoy is leaving London secretly late tomorrow night, will you?"

The Viscount's reply was unexpectedly harsh. "Are you hoping to set up an assassination attempt, by any chance?"

Mr Travers managed to sound convincingly horrified, although a hint of colour appeared along his cheekbones. "Why the devil should you think such a thing, James? Nothing further from my thoughts, I promise you."

The Viscount studied his friend from beneath hooded lids, the tautness of his mouth betraying the apparent laziness of his eyes. "I shall let Marie-Rose know that the Russians have reached complete agreement with the War Minister," he said. "Don't expect me to pass on any precise information about the movements of the Russian envoy."

Arthur Travers did not attempt to argue, but simply reached for his hat and cane. "No wonder nobody is ever able to persuade you to take a position in the government," he said. "You really are the most uncomfortable fellow to have as a friend, James. Can't think why I continue to tolerate you."

"It's my brandy," said the Viscount. "You know it's the best in town. My grandfather had many splendid qualities, but his taste in wine was definitely the best of them."

Arthur Travers paused at the front door. "I shall come and beg another glass from you as soon as you are back in town. Send me word when you arrive."

The Earl of Ashbourne placed the tips of his fingers neatly together and inspected his son. "You may sit down, James. I am overwhelmed, even if you are not, by the unexpected honour of receiving two visits from you in a single month."

The Viscount's outward composure did not betray a crack. "Thank you, sir," he said, and sat down in the chair his father indicated. "I have come because I have some news which I believe will please you."

The Earl's penetrating gaze was removed from the tips of his fingers to his son's face. "You perceive me all attention, my dear James."

"I have come to tell you of my betrothal," the Viscount said. "Miss Adrienne Abbott, the younger daughter of Sir George Abbott, has accepted my proposal. Her father has given his approval. I hope, sir, to receive your blessing on the match."

The Earl's eyes flickered slightly. "You have succeeded in surprising me, James."

"Favourably, sir, I trust."

"Adrienne Abbott," the Earl mused. "Daughter of Sir George … And I believe her mother was Pamela Slade, was she not?"

"Lady Abbott's family is from Gloucestershire, sir."

"Yes, yes. You have chosen one of Pamela Slade's daughters. She was a very beautiful woman." A faint smile touched his lips. "Congratulations, James, you have made a most respectable choice. I shall look forward to welcoming Miss Abbott and her family on a visit to Ashbourne. Or perhaps we may come up to town. Your mother would be delighted for an excuse to escape from Ashbourne."

The Viscount was alarmed at this unexpected enthusiasm for a family reunion with his betrothed. "Well, sir, I dare say a visit could be arranged nearer the time of our wedding. If you please, sir, I should now like to discuss the arrangements for the return of my estate."

The Earl raised his eyebrows in interrogation. "I am not sure that I understand what needs to be discussed?"

The Viscount swallowed his impatience. "I cannot discuss marriage settlements with Sir George," he said, "when the major part of my assets is being held by you."

"I do not perceive your difficulty, James. You may refer the matter to our family lawyers. I don't suppose Sir George will expect to sit across a table from you and haggle over terms."

"But what will my lawyer do about Cravensleigh?"

The Earl looked at his son, before returning his gaze to the papers placed in orderly piles upon the desk. "Our lawyer, James, will inform Sir George's lawyer, that the estate of Cravensleigh will be returned to you and the new Viscountess Cravensleigh on the day of your marriage. He will hold the deeds in trust until that day. You may think of Cravensleigh as my wedding gift to you and Miss Abbott. It will be delivered to you clear of all mortgages."

The Viscount could barely restrain himself until his father had finished speaking. He sprang to his feet and, by clenching his teeth almost shut, managed to hold back the shout of rage. "I don't want Cravensleigh delivered free of all mortgages on my wedding day! I need it *now*, and I am prepared to pay the interest in order to have it." By a great effort of will he managed to moderate his voice even further. "I understand why you took Cravensleigh from me," the Viscount said. "I admit it was an error of judgment to gamble with such an important part of my inheritance. Believe me, sir, the error will not be repeated."

"I shall do my best to see that it is not. When we buy an inferior horse at an inflated price, Cravensleigh, we may term that act an *error of judgment*. A man who gambles away his inheritance does not make a mistake. He betrays a trust. I imagine, since I have never had cause to doubt your intelligence, that you are able to perceive the distinction." He turned back to his desk, removed pens and papers from the drawer, and proceeded to write a letter. The Viscount could feel his nerves stretching thinner with every scratch of the quill across the paper. "Here," the Earl said at last, "please give this brief note to Sir George when you return to town. I have no doubt your mother will wish to write a similar expression of good wishes to Lady Abbott and to her daughter."

The Viscount took the proffered letter. "You are entirely too generous, sir." He didn't try to keep the irony from his voice.

"Probably," his father agreed. "But I trust I am not a fool. Engagements can be broken, James, and I intend to see you married. How long you have to wait for your estate depends upon how long *you* wait before you make Miss Abbott your wife. As far as I am concerned, you may be married next week. And I've no doubt that your mother and sister would swoon with ecstasy at the thought of your wedding."

"I don't think Miss Abbott wishes for an early wedding, sir."

"Does she not? That is most unusual for a woman." He smiled to indicate that, as far as he was concerned, the subject of a marriage date was closed. "Please join me in a glass of burgundy, James. You have a long journey back to town tomorrow, and no doubt a busy time once you get there. Do, please, keep us informed of how your affairs progress. Your mother will need at least three weeks to provide herself with a suitable dress."

The Viscount took the glass of burgundy and walked casually across to the window. It was easier to deceive his father if he wasn't forced to look into those penetrating grey eyes. "I expect I shall be able to persuade Miss Abbott to agree to an early wedding," he said with a careless shrug of his shoulders. "If I can organise a family betrothal party, I hope you and my mother will be able to attend?"

"You may count upon it, James." The Viscount detected some undercurrent of amusement in his father's voice, but he didn't dare to turn round in order to check his suspicions. "In fact," said the Earl, "I can safely say that almost nothing would keep us away!"

The Viscount drove back to London with a reckless disregard for his own safety and very little regard for the safety of anybody else who was unlucky enough to be on the road. After a narrow escape from a head-on collision with the Dover mailcoach, Denby reached out and touched his master's arm.

"I have no wish to die, m'lord, so please slow down or hand them reins over to me."

For a moment the Viscount regarded his servant with white-lipped fury, then there was an infinitesimal relaxation of the headlong pace. "I'm sorry," he said brusquely.

This time there was no halting for refreshment at a wayside inn. The curricle was stopped only to change horses and the new team was raced into London as fast as the Viscount could urge them over the road. However, their break-neck pace slowed at the approach of every blind corner and Denby knew his reproof had been heeded.

The Viscount scarcely broke the silence of their journey until they were back inside his London home. Denby started to lay out clean clothes for his master, selecting the informal evening wear suitable for a dinner with the Comtesse de la Ronde. Whatever his private thoughts about the Comtesse, Denby knew his master's patterns of behaviour well enough by now.

"Not those!" Denby was startled when the Viscount's words cut through the silent room. "There's still time for me to get to Almack's tonight. Find me the proper outfit, will you, Denby?"

"Almack's?" Deny repeated the word as if he had never heard mention of the famous club. "*You* are going to Almack's, my lord?"

There was a certain wryness to the Viscount's expression. "Why not, Denby? I believe I still have an admission card."

"Why, yes, of course, my lord. I will … I'll fetch your knee-breeches and silk stockings right away, m'lord."

The Viscount arrived at Almack's only minutes before the doors closed at eleven o'clock. He couldn't remember when he had last sought admission to this citadel of social propriety. Neither, it seemed, could anybody else. If his temper had been less frayed, he might have been diverted by the hush which greeted his arrival. There ought to have been a certain cynical amusement to be derived from the knowledge that he could command such awestruck attention merely by behaving in strict accordance with the conventions. As it was, his mood was too uneven to find the sudden silence, the fading away of the buzz of chatter, at all gratifying. His face whitened with the strain of keeping rigid control over his facial expression. His eyes swept impatiently around the room.

He caught sight of Adrienne almost at once. She was dancing the quadrille with a handsome young man, smiling and looking very well entertained. She and her partner seemed to be the only people in the room who hadn't noticed his arrival. His mood darkened even further.

He made his way across the floor, inclining his head briefly in the direction of some of his friends, his expression forbidding in the extreme. Lady Abbott found her eyes riveted to the sinuous power of his black-clad figure and she shivered with a curious mixture of pride and anxiety. Maternal pride triumphed when she saw that the Viscount was making straight for her chair, publicly proclaiming that he had come to Almack's just for Adrienne's sake. With difficulty she restrained herself from turning and giving the assembled company a triumphant bow. She contented herself with raising her hand and saying graciously, "My dear Viscount, I am pleased to see that you have returned safely from your visit to Ashbourne."

"Lady Abbott." He bowed courteously over her hand, but didn't oblige her by recounting what had transpired with his father. He turned round suddenly as Adrienne came off the dance-floor, and Lady Abbot saw his speech die away as he looked at her daughter. For some reason his mouth thinned into grimness.

"Miss Abbott," he said peremptorily, "I believe the next set of dances must be promised to me."

The merriment faded from Adrienne's face. "I am tired," she said coolly, her voice reflecting none of the anger that the Viscount could see sparkling in her eyes. "You must excuse me, my lord." She paused for a fraction of a second before saying, "May I introduce my brother to you? This is Peter Abbott, who has just returned from an extended stay in Ireland. Peter, this is Viscount Cravensleigh."

The Viscount shook hands with the handsome young man, irritated that he had not spotted the resemblance between Adrienne and her partner. Irrationally, his resentment turned towards Adrienne. He smiled, but not in a way that removed any of the ice from his eyes.

"Even if you are tired," he said, "I cannot bear to be deprived of your company. If you are too weary to dance, Miss Abbott, we must go in search of some refreshments." Before she could protest, he placed a firm hand beneath her elbow. "Mr Abbott will take good care of your mother, I am sure." Without waiting for a reply, he swept a deep bow and led Adrienne firmly in the direction of the dining-salon.

The Viscount found two relatively secluded chairs and wondered how people were supposed to have private conversations when surrounded by an audience of fifty or so people, all partaking of the somewhat spartan supply of refreshments.

"Would you care for some lemonade, Miss Abbott?"

"Thank you, my lord, but I am not thirsty."

"I have just returned from Ashbourne," he said, abandoning his desultory attempt at polite conversation. "My father has given his blessing to the match and I should like to make a formal announcement of our betrothal tomorrow." He tried to speak casually, as if it had been agreed all along that their betrothal would soon become public knowledge.

The colour rose swiftly into her cheeks and then receded, leaving her paler than before. "My lord, you *know* we cannot announce a betrothal that only exists in our imaginations. I don't know what I was thinking of that day in the Park! We were both temporarily insane to consider such a foolish scheme. We must stop this charade before it proceeds any further."

He was far too angry to hear the panic lying behind her words. "Oh, yes!" he said. In his attempt to control the level of his voice, the words emerged as an angry hiss. "It would no doubt suit you very well to cry off now! I suppose Mr Bagley has left town and you feel there is no longer any danger of receiving an offer from him. Well, unfortunately, Miss Abbott, it doesn't suit me to cry off the match just at the moment, and I imagine *you* will have a hard time persuading your family to turn down such a splendid catch as I!"

"Your attitude is insufferable!" she breathed. "We never agreed to a wedding. We agreed only to a private betrothal and you promised it would never be publicly announced." She struggled visibly to regain her calm. "Come, my lord. Let us put an end to this masquerade tonight. There will be some personal unpleasantness for us both, but no major problems, if we simply tell our families that we no longer wish to think of ourselves as betrothed to one another."

He replied through clenched teeth. "Twenty thousand pounds a year may seem a minor problem to you, Miss Abbott, but I confess to being rather more mercenary in my attitudes. I have a sordid attachment to the comforts of life and I wish to enjoy the income from my estates. To do that, my father says I must marry. You have already agreed to become my bride. Your family and mine have given their approval to the match. Why should it not be announced?"

Her eyes blazed with anger. For a moment he felt his breath catch in his throat as she turned upon him with the full force of her fury. "You tricked me," she said. "When you were pretending to help me, you just *tricked* me."

"No!" Too late, he saw how disastrously he had managed his plea for help. "No," he repeated more quietly. "Miss Abbott ... Adrienne ... I didn't lie to you. I had no intention of forcing you into an unwelcome marriage." He glanced round the room which still seemed full of people all pretending they were totally uninterested in the whispered conversation being conducted between the two of them.

"Hell and damnation!" he swore beneath his breath. "How can I explain things to you when we can never be alone?"

She was touched by his genuine frustration as she would not have been by a polished request for help. "What did your father say that has set you so on edge, my lord?" She wouldn't admit, even to herself, that her anger had started to cool as soon as he whispered her name.

The Viscount's mouth curled into a grimace of self-derision. "My father has the insight and cunning instincts of a trained hunter. He also cherishes a less than flattering opinion of my morals. He suspected a trap as soon as I told him of our engagement. He guessed that I would refuse to go ahead with the wedding ceremony once I had regained my estate."

She stared down at her fingers, clasped tightly together in her lap. "So your father won't return Cravensleigh to you until you are actually married?" she asked.

"Unfortunately, that seems to be the case. On the day of our wedding, my father will see that the deeds are handed over to me." Unthinkingly, he took her hands into his own. "Adrienne, couldn't you consider marrying me? It would be a marriage of convenience for both of us. I swear I would make no demands upon you, and put no restraints upon the way you wish to conduct yourself."

She suppressed the tiny thrill she felt when she

heard the urgent pleading in his voice. The chill words of his final sentences struck home just in time to prevent her committing herself to an irretrievable folly.

"No!" she exclaimed. She got to her feet, so that she could no longer listen to temptation. "No, my lord. We can't base our lives on trickery. Marriage is a serious commitment, not a game to be twisted to suit our momentary whims." To her intense relief, she saw that her brother had arrived in the dining-salon. For once she blessed her mother's rigid sense of propriety that would not allow any private conversation to last for more than a few minutes. "Hello, Peter," she said with determined cheerfulness. "Have you come to join us? Or do you bring a message from my mother?"

"Our mother wishes to return home," he said, smiling affectionately at his sister. "You will forgive the interruption, my lord?" The remark was courteously spoken, but the Viscount knew he would have no further opportunities to speak privately to Adrienne that night.

He followed Adrienne and her brother from the dining-salon, seething with a mixture of anger and frustration. Buried deep within the rage he was conscious of the faint stirrings of another emotion. He walked beside Peter and Adrienne, forced into an appearance of conventional conversation, while every nerve in his body felt aware of the potential passion contained behind the rigid exterior Adrienne presented to the world.

The Viscount and Adrienne arrived back at Lady Abbott's side. They all parted with the politest of meaningless phrases. Inside, Adrienne and the Viscount simmered with the twin emotions of anger and despair.

CHAPTER
SIX

As soon as the Viscount entered her bedroom the Comtesse de la Ronde could see that he was in the blackest of moods. She opened her arms in a gesture of greeting, gliding quickly across the thick carpets to welcome him. She was secretly pleased to observe the fury lurking at the back of his eyes. Angry men, as she well knew, tended to be rash in their confidences. She tossed her head back and gave him a warm smile, knowing that her long hair gleamed in the flattering softness of the candlelight, and that her body moved with the lithe and sinuous grace of a young girl's.

"*Mon cher Vicomte* ..." She finished her welcome with a teasing kiss. "How fortunate that I have just ordered the servants to open a bottle of champagne. Here, take some, so that you may lift that horrid frown from between your eyes." She gave an enchanting little pout. "You are so formal tonight, *mon cher*. Where have you been in knee-breeches and silk stockings?"

"Almack's," he said and accepted the brimming glass of champagne. He touched his lips to the wrist she turned up for his kiss. "Marie-Rose," he said, changing the subject. "You look bewitching tonight." If she had not looked closely at his eyes, if she had not been so experienced with men, she would never have suspected the anger which simmered beneath the cool surface and the flirtatious voice.

She twirled round in an enticing swirl of lace and transparent silk. "It is my new robe-de-chambre that you find so alluring, no?" She sank into a curtsy at his feet, allowing the loose folds of her gown to fall apart. She was naked beneath the shimmering dressing-gown.

The Viscount tossed the glass of champagne down his throat in a single gulp and reached for her with sudden urgency. He thrust her body against his own, crushing her to him in a passionate embrace.

"No," he said curtly. "It is not your clothes that I like. It is your body which I find so desirable." He pushed the gown further from her shoulders and carried her towards the bed, tearing at the folds of his cravat as he did so.

She was excited by his evident impatience, but when he would have flung himself down beside her, she warded him off and put an admonitory finger against his lips. "You are very ferocious tonight. Who has made you so angry?"

"It is nothing," he said. "Don't talk, Marie-Rose. Your lips were made to be kissed."

She submitted willingly, feeling the thrill of passion he could always arouse in her no matter how hard she tried to remain aloof. She wanted to relax in his embrace and forget the pointless political struggles between his country and her own. But the loyalty she felt towards her native land, the hidden resentments caused by years of exile, would not allow her to surrender completely to his touch. She forced herself to wriggle away from him, wrapping the folds of lace once more across her body.

"You need some more champagne," she whispered. "You are still too angry to think of making love." She closed her eyes and executed a frightened shiver that was not wholly pretence. "In this mood, you are … too wild … for me." Through the flutter of her half-closed eyelashes, she watched his expression, pulling herself off the bed just before he could push her back down against the pillows.

With seductive hands, she removed his jacket, ruffling her fingers beneath the thin linen of his shirt. "See how your heart is beating!" she exclaimed softly. "Feel!" She took his hand beneath her own and pressed it against his chest. Her other hand smoothed the frown on his brow with the light touch of a butterfly. "Who makes you so cross with the world? Could it be the boring English virgin whom you are going to marry?"

Even as she spoke, he jerked away from her touch and walked over to the table where the servants had placed the champagne. He drank two glasses in quick succession before he returned to her side.

"Why should I think of boring subjects such as marriage when I am with you?" he said at last. "If I am preoccupied, it is because of events at the War Office. Castlereagh has been closeted with the secret envoy from the Russian Tsar for the past week, and I haven't spoken to him for days. I am hoping that I shall not have to wait for too much longer before Castlereagh remembers that I am in town and waiting on his pleasure. You know – I have told you before – that I am sent for only when the Minister starts to worry about events in the Peninsula. Then Castlereagh recalls that I hold an honorary position on his staff *and* I have actually visited Portugal and Spain." He laughed cynically. "They have very adaptable memories at the Ministry. While they are asking my advice and telling me their plans, they conveniently forget that I am supposed to be the liaison between King George and the Secretary for War. God knows, nobody expects me to report anything back to the King or his Court. If there is one single thing that the Foreign Office and the War Office agree upon, it is the fact that the King should be kept ignorant of everything that is going on."

"Tell me about this Russian envoy. Has his mission here been entirely successful?"

"I believe so." The Viscount looked at her through narrowed eyes. Marie-Rose was disconcerted by the sudden, cold shrewdness that replaced the former passion in his expression. "Why should you care about a Russian envoy, Marie-Rose? We have better things to do than talk about the machinations of the Russian government, have we not?"

She already regretted the direct question. She knew from past experience that the Viscount never responded as she wished. She bit her lip in silent frustration, then swayed against him in a burst of unfeigned passion.

"Do not trouble yourself, *mon cher*," she breathed. "I shall soon make you forget that Castlereagh exists. I will even make you forget that you have a new and boring fiancée."

He gave a strange laugh. "Will you, Marie-Rose?" With sudden savagery, he flung her down on to the bed, indifferent to the rip of her lace flounces. "I hope so," he said. "I hope so indeed."

She just had time to think that she would charge the French government for a new frill of Alençon lace before the demands of her body made all thought impossible.

The Viscount found little pleasure in the Comtesse's bed. His thoughts had developed an aggravating tendency to stray from the supposed attractions of the woman in his arms. They fixed themselves instead upon the supposed deficiencies of the infuriating and unco-operative Adrienne Abbott. Marie-Rose seemed to observe nothing amiss in their passionate encounter, but the Viscount found he was haunted by the memory of a pair of angry violet eyes.

He was dressing, and flirting somewhat mechanically with Marie-Rose, when the realisation dawned upon him that he could force Adrienne to marry him. Her parents would give her no chance to cry off once the betrothal was public knowledge. All he needed to do, therefore, was to insert the announcement of their betrothal in the *Morning Post* and the solution to his financial problems would inevitably follow.

Viscount Cravensleigh left his mistress's boudoir with unflattering eagerness and walked straight home to compose the formal announcement of his betrothal. A footman was dispatched with the notice and a small pouch of golden coins to ensure that the news of the betrothal was inserted in the very next issue of the *Morning Post*.

If the Viscount was aware of an uncomfortable feeling of betrayal as he finished composing his flowing phrases he told himself that he merely regretted the necessity for taking a wife – any wife. He drowned his troublesome conscience in a surfeit of alcohol, and staggered up to bed as dawn was turning the sky pink. He did not sleep very well, but during the uncomfortable hours of restless slumber he managed to convince himself that his gloomy mood was caused by annoyance at the prospect of facing up to an imminent marriage. By the time Denby brought in his morning coffee, and a copy of the newspaper, the

Viscount had persuaded himself that his lingering qualms were quite unnecessary. His wide experience with women told him that they all looked forward to the prospect of marrying well, and a future Earl with a sizeable potential income had to be considered a notable prize. Miss Abbott, surely, would soon learn to congratulate herself upon the twists of fate that had captured her such an eligible husband.

The Viscount sipped his coffee and pointed out the betrothal notice to Denby. The servant offered enthusiastic congratulations and the Viscount reclined against the pillows with an increasing sensation of satisfaction. It was foolish to feel he had tricked Miss Abbott. Neither he nor Adrienne wished to endure the hypocrisy of a conventional marriage and she would soon understand the advantages of this match for both of them. Indeed, the Viscount decided taking a healthy bite out of his morning toast, she would soon thank him for taking the initiative in making a public announcement of their betrothal.

He sprang out of bed. He would go and explain in person to Adrienne just why this marriage was such a good idea.

"Fetch me my new grey jacket, Denby," he said. "I have an urgent call to pay upon my fiancée."

"My love, my love! Such excellent news ... The announcement has been made already! How elegantly he has phrased it. How superior it looks expressed in print!" Adrienne looked up from her silent consumption of breakfast, an occupation which had not, in any case, been giving her much pleasure. She was filled with an immediate and dreadful foreboding. "What looks superior in print, Mama?" she asked urgently.

Lady Abbott was far too happy to observe that Adrienne's words expressed none of her own effervescent pleasure.

"Why, the announcement of your betrothal, my dearest child! Here it is, in this morning's newspaper, and we thought it would be another week at least before everything was ready for a public declaration!" With smug satisfaction she read out loud.

" *'A marriage has been arranged and will shortly take place between Adrienne Jane de Vere Abbott, younger daughter of Sir George Abbott, Bart., of Abbott's Grange in the County of Wiltshire, and James George Beaulieu Ashbourne, sixth Viscount Cravensleigh, eldest son of James, seventh Earl of Ashbourne …'* And so on, and so on. I declare I have never seen a wedding announcement that looked so handsome."

"Give me the newspaper!" Adrienne grabbed the newspaper then recalled her manners just in time. "That is to say, if you please, Mama." She scanned the paragraph with her initial expression of disbelief turning rapidly to anger. She threw the paper down on to the table and Lady Abbott snatched it up in distress. "Take care, Adrienne! You have covered the Viscount's announcement with marmalade!"

"I wish that I had covered the *Viscount* with marmalade!" said Adrienne succinctly. "Or perhaps with tar and feathers. Isn't that what the Americans do to traitors?"

Lady Abbott wrinkled her brow in the direction of her daughter, then gave a delicate shrug.

"Dear Adrienne. It's so long since you last said anything that I understood that I've given up expecting to make head or tail of your conversation. You been in love with a man for weeks and now we read the announcement of your marriage. Are you happy, as any normal female would be? No! You throw the newspaper on the table and start discussing the extraordinary customs of the American rebels! Sometimes I worry in case your mind has become quite overbalanced by the pressure of all those masculine lessons you took with your brother. Everybody *knows* that the female constitution cannot absorb the same quantity of knowledge as the male!'' Her chin wobbled uncertainly. "It's all my fault, and Sir George will never forgive me! He warned me how it would be. I finally manage to bring you to the point of accepting an offer of marriage – and such a splendid match – and now you are off on one of your strange starts again!'' Two fat tears rolled down her cheeks. "I was planning to have a delightful day buying wedding clothes and now I have to spend all morning worrying in case you tell the Viscount that the Americans should have tarred and feathered him! And he will never understand that you mean no harm by it. I don't suppose he's ever had to put up with a clever female in *his* family ... After all, everybody knows the Ashbournes can trace their ancestry straight back to William the Conqueror.''

"And that, I suppose, must be considered an infallible guarantee of feeble-mindedness,'' said Adrienne. She saw that more tears were forming at the corner of her mother's eyes and she was overcome by remorse. "Don't cry, Mama! Please, there is no need for you to feel unhappy. Viscount Cravensleigh and I are going to deal extremely well together, I promise you. And I haven't the faintest doubt that you will manage to produce the wedding of the season. And remember it will be for the second year in a row. What a triumph for you!''

Lady Abbott's tears immediately ceased, to be

replaced by a beaming smile. "Dearest child! I knew you would be sensible in the end. Now let me see, do you think we should go to St Katharine's warehouse, or do you think somewhere in Pall Mall would be better? The silk in Mr Swan's emporium is always of such an excellent quality, don't you agree?"

"Perhaps we should go to two or three different places," suggested Adrienne, with a generosity that was not lost upon her mother. It was usually a labour of Hercules to coax Adrienne inside one warehouse, let alone two or three in a single afternoon. Lady Abbott gave her daughter a beaming smile.

"There is just one thing, Mama. Could I ... would you permit me to speak to Viscount Cravensleigh alone before we go shopping?"

"Are you expecting him to call? Did he make some private assignation when he was talking to you last night at Almack's?"

"Oh, no!" said Adrienne. "But I think we should discuss some of the details of our marriage, don't you? There are so many arrangements still to be made."

"It is true that we ought to settle upon a date for the ceremony as soon as possible," Lady Abbott said. "And we should also make plans for a betrothal party. Yes, yes. I think I shall send a footman round to the Viscount's house and request him to pay us a call."

"And may I speak to him alone?"

Lady Abbott permitted herself a tender sigh. "Ah, the impatience of you young lovers! I shall permit you to speak to the Viscount alone for fifteen minutes, but that is all, Adrienne. The betrothal has been announced, but that is no reason for us to become slipshod in our standards. Delicacy and modesty are feminine virtues which can never be overrated."

"Yes, Mama. Thank you, Mama." Adrienne

dropped a light kiss on her mother's cheek. "I am truly grateful to you."

"Dear child!" Lady Abbott's brief moment of unhappiness was quite forgotten. "How fortunate that the season is not quite ended. There is Lady Bennett-Smythe's party tonight. How delightful it will be! So many people still in town and they will all have read the announcement. You must wear your new rose-pink silk. It is rather low cut, but then you're not a girl fresh from the schoolroom any more."

"No, I'm not," Adrienne agreed. She gave a tiny, hollow laugh. "It seems I'm about to become a Viscountess."

The Viscount, despite his earlier rationalisations, read Lady Abbott's request to call with considerable misgiving. However, he consoled himself with the thought that women, after all, were created to live under the guidance of their menfolk. If Adrienne still felt any opposition to the match, it would no doubt soon wither under the force of his superior reasoning.

He gave a final adjustment to the folds of his cravat and stood patiently while Denby eased his shoulders into his new coat of grey Bath superfine. The valet was so delighted with his master's betrothal that he could hardly contain his stream of good wishes and sage advice. The Viscount thought cynically that his father and his valet seemed equal believers in the benefits of matrimony. He spared a pessimistic moment to wonder why, with all the eligible girls in London, he had managed to get himself entangled with the only one who wasn't enthralled at the prospect of a wedding.

His mood was still uncertain when, less than an hour later, he was ushered into Lady Abbott's presence.

"My dear Viscount!" she smiled at him playfully. "You are a naughty man not to have warned us of what we should read in our newspapers this morning! But, as Sir George said, it was handsomely written, most handsome indeed!"

The Viscount bowed. "I trust I am forgiven, by you and by Sir George? Once my father had added his approval to your own, there seemed to be no reason for delay."

"Not the least in the world, I'm sure you are right, and Adrienne will soon understand … That is to say … Ah!" Lady Abbott could not hold back the sigh of relief. "Here is my little Adrienne herself, come to greet you on this happy day!"

Adrienne, who was a good three inches taller than her mother, walked into the drawing-room looking neither little nor happy. She had brushed her hair high on her head in a smooth style that made absolutely no concession to the demands of fashion. She hadn't attempted to induce a single curl in her naturally straight hair, and the severe style revealed the classical lines of her neck and the austere perfection of her high cheekbones. The Viscount caught his breath involuntarily at the sight of such simple elegance. He found it hard to tear his eyes away from her pale face and slender figure.

She had chosen to wear a white muslin morning-gown which reminded the Viscount of some fragile ice-crystals he had once seen suspended high on a German mountainside. He felt an unaccountable urge to seize her in his arms and melt the ice-encrusted exterior with the force of his own passion. He was quite shaken when he realised that he had been so intent on watching Adrienne's every small movement that he hadn't heard what Lady Abbott was saying. He spoke quickly, to fill the silence which had fallen upon their group.

"Miss Abbott ..." He took her hand into his own with a gesture of formal affection. She looked so utterly unmoved that he was surprised to feel her fingers shake within his clasp.

"You look wonderfully cool, Miss Abbott, on such a hot summer's day."

"Thank you." Her voice betrayed no emotion. "It was good of you to call."

"Indeed, yes," Lady Abbott said, hastening to cover up her daughter's lack of enthusiasm. "I requested you to pay us a visit, my dear Viscount, because we need to set a date for the betrothal party. Even more important, we must consider a day for the wedding ceremony itself." She beamed at the silent couple, then sighed. The modern generation had such an extraordinary way of showing happiness.

"I am all eagerness to set a date for our marriage," the Viscount said. "I believe no date could be too soon for me." He smiled with devastating charm towards Lady Abbott and gave Adrienne a little bow, his manner at its most debonair.

She looked at him directly, just for a moment, out of stony eyes, before her gaze was once more fixed upon the middle distance. "How about next summer?" she suggested. "I believe that allows me sufficient time to make the necessary mental adjustments."

"Adrienne!" exclaimed her mother, but she was interrupted by the smooth voice of the Viscount. "You are teasing both of us, my dear Miss Abbott. I know you wouldn't expect my loving heart to wait for more than a year to claim you."

Adrienne gave him another brief, scornful look. "Oh, no," she said. "I wouldn't wish to keep any man waiting if he loved me."

"How sweet!" said Lady Abbott, who wasn't at all sure that her daughter's remark was as gracious as it sounded. "I shall go and tell Sir George that the Viscount is here, Adrienne. You two young lovebirds can work out a date for the ceremony while I am gone. Viscount Cravensleigh, will you excuse me for ten minutes or so?"

He raised her hand to his lips, bowing punctiliously until she was out of the drawing-room. As a truly exceptional gesture of goodwill, she closed the heavy double doors behind her. Adrienne and the Viscount were temporarily alone.

He cleared his throat portentously, not wanting her to say anything before he had a chance to start his explanations. "Miss Abbott, I am grateful to have this opportunity to speak with you privately. I trust you are not displeased with the course events have taken?"

"Not displeased!" She swung away from him, her hands clenched into tight fists of frustration at her sides. "I begged Mama to let me see you alone. I hoped you would tell me this was all a dreadful mistake, some sort of a waking nightmare." For a moment colour flooded into her cheeks. "How could you?" she asked. "How could you betray me? I *trusted* you!"

He walked over to her side, pushing down the feelings of guilt. "Miss Abbott ... Adrienne ... I believe it will be best for both of us in the end. You know my father will only return Cravensleigh to me when I am married, and you ... Well, you have to marry somebody, so why should it not be me?"

She whirled round to face him at last, her face white but her eyes blazing with anger. "Why should it not be you?" she repeated. "Did it never occur to you in your arrogance that there might be other men I would prefer to marry if I had to pick a husband?"

The Viscount felt a surge of anger, all the more acute because it was so strongly tinged with guilt. All his private resolutions about explaining the situation calmly and quietly flew out of the window. "No, Miss Abbott, such a thought had not occurred to me." He realised he was shouting and lowered his voice. "I am a man of the world, not a green boy and I know how to value my assets. I am offering you an income of twenty thousand pounds a year and the prospect of an ancient and noble title. I am not hunchbacked, I do not limp, I have the use of all my faculties. Why should I suppose that you would find me unattractive as a husband? Most of the women in London will be sick with envy, I can assure you."

"Then perhaps we could arrange for one of those women to cure her sickness by changing places with me! The Comtesse de la Ronde, perhaps?" She bit off her remark almost before it was uttered but it was too late.

"She, at least, knows how a woman should behave! Unfortunately, as a gentleman, I cannot withdraw my offer for your hand."

"As a gentleman!" she gasped, and then fell silent, afraid that she was hovering on the borderline of hysteria. "Oh, what is the use!" she exclaimed. "We both know that I shall be forced to marry you. But I will never forgive you for what you have done to me, my lord. You will discover hatred makes an uncomfortable foundation for marriage."

"Hatred, Miss Abbott, can flow in two directions. If you have finished your childish outbursts, perhaps we could now set a date for our wedding ceremony."

"Oh, my lord, I have explained everything so badly! You cannot possibly want to marry me."

"We neither of us look forward to married life, Miss Abbott. Perhaps we are fortunate in that we shall be spared the disillusion that follows so many wedding ceremonies. Our opinion of each other could hardly sink any further, I am sure you will agree."

She tried one final plea. "Surely even twenty thousand pounds a year isn't enough to reward you for a lifetime tied to a woman whom you dislike?"

He shrugged. "I would marry worse bargains than yourself, Miss Abbott, in order to regain Cravensleigh. May I suggest three weeks next Friday for our wedding? I believe that allows time for essential arrangements to be made."

"Three weeks!" She laughed hysterically. "You seem anxious to start your term of penal servitude!"

"Happiness in marriage, Miss Abbott, is surely not the object of this exercise for either of us."

"How can we live together, day in and day out, when there is so much ill-feeling between us?"

"I have it on excellent authority, Madam, that society does not expect a man to spend more than one month a year in the company of his wife. I think we may learn to endure each other's foibles for four weeks out of the fifty-two, don't you agree? Provided that you keep up your pretty pretence of conforming to the conventions, you will never be able to complain that my demands upon you are burdensome."

"No," she said. "I believe that I will not." She fell silent, since her tongue seemed to be frozen along with the rest of her body. Once it had seemed to her that in the Viscount she had found a friend. Now the fragile beginnings of that friendship had been ruined, to be replaced by misunderstandings and scorn.

"Is there anything further for us to discuss?" she asked in a low voice. If the Viscount hadn't been so angry he would have heard the pain hidden in her simple question.

"I think you have managed to cover all the ground quite effectively, Miss Abbott. Perhaps you would prefer to withdraw now and leave me to deal with your father alone? Convention requires, does it not, that you should feign disinterest in the sordid details of the financial settlements your father and I will have to make."

"Yes," she said. "Convention sometimes thrusts unlikely roles upon all of us." She curtsied and held out her hand in a brief gesture of farewell. "We shall no doubt be forced to see a considerable amount of one another over the next few weeks. I shall strive to live up to all the expectations you have for your future Viscountess. In return, I wish you would keep all private discourse between us to an absolute minimum."

"It will be my pleasure to comply, Miss Abbott. If you can please my parents and keep out of my way, you will exceed the highest hopes I have ever entertained about the performance of my wife."

She was stung by the cold cynicism of his reply. "And in exchange?" she cried out. "What is to be my reward from this marriage?"

"You, my dear, will be Viscountess Cravensleigh, and mistress of twenty thousand pounds per annum. Is that not sufficient compensation for the sacrifice of a few romantic dreams?"

CHAPTER
SEVEN

The Comtesse de la Ronde did not hold a very high opinion of the married state. Her practical French upbringing ensured that she was, from an early age, aware of the gulf between the felicitous state of being in love and the dull state of preparing for matrimony. Her experience as the wife of an aged and exiled aristocrat did nothing to alter her childhood opinions, and her experience as the mistress of several married men merely strengthened her suspicion that the institution of marriage was considerably more agreeable for men than for women. The rules for the game of matrimony, she decided, were long on wifely duties but disagreeably short on the subject of wifely privilege.

In these circumstances, the printed announcement of the Viscount's betrothal should not have been a matter of any concern to her, but she read the notice in the *Morning Post* in grim silence. She was shocked to find her hands gripping the newspaper with a ferocity that turned her knuckles white and crumpled the pages of the paper to the point of illegibility. Since she was not in the habit of deceiving herself about the true state of her own emotions, she was able to identify as jealousy the feeling which raged through her when she read the news.

It was less easy to imagine what she could do about a situation which fell outside the scope of her previous emotional experience. She had never been in love before, but she knew that she felt threatened by the existence of a future Viscountess Cravensleigh. She was seized by an urgent need to meet the unknown Miss Abbott, and to judge for herself how much of a problem the Viscount's wife was likely to be.

She walked downstairs and picked up Lady Bennett-Smythe's invitation card which, as she had remembered, rested on the inlaid silver tray in her drawing-room. In the past, the Comtesse had avoided parties where her presence might cause embarrassment either to her hostess or to her fellow guests. Such discretion had paid rewards, for she retained her place on the fringes of the *haut ton*, a position that was necessary for both her professions: useful information and useful lovers were most easily discovered within the drawing-rooms of London society.

Tonight, however, the Comtesse cast discretion aside. The desire to see Miss Abbott overcame caution. She presented herself at Lady Bennett-Smythe's house promptly at nine o'clock and proceeded through the Bennett-Smythe drawing-rooms, exchanging greetings with her acquaintances just as if there was nothing remarkable about her presence at the reception on the very night of her lover's betrothal.

Lady Bennett-Smythe's guests sat back and waited eagerly for the arrival of Miss Abbott and Viscount Cravensleigh. Surely the presence of a notorious rake (possibly reformed?), a beautiful mistress and a prospective bride ought to provide the jaded palates of the *ton* with at least one tempting morsel of scandal?

Society was kept in suspense until after ten o'clock, when Miss Abbott finally arrived in the company of her mother, her brother and her fiancé. She wore a low-cut gown of rose pink silk, and her normally pale cheeks were suffused with an attractive flush of colour. Lady Abbott, regally draped in striped golden satin, looked as triumphant as was possible for a matron doing nothing more extraordinary than greeting her hostess and bowing to some of her friends. Society bore Lady Abbott no ill-will for her unconcealed air of victory. She had, after all, achieved the seemingly impossible and brought Cravensleigh up to scratch. The Viscount himself was attired entirely in black, whether as a reflection of his mood or in deference to Miss Abbott's choice of rose-pink, Society could not decide. He looked much as he always did, which was to say highly desirable as a lover and exceptionally dangerous as potential husband-material.

The progress of this interesting party into the main reception room was watched closely by not less than a hundred pairs of eyes. Regrettably, the Viscount and Miss Abbott did nothing more gossip-provoking than talking to some of their friends and sitting down to a long conversation with the Duchess of Exeter. Society's expectations settled once again upon the Comtesse de la Ronde, whose bright laughter surely seemed somewhat forced since the imposing entrance of Lady Abbott and her party.

Adrienne was only too well aware of the interested speculation which followed the movements of her party. She was also acutely aware of the Comtesse de la Ronde, who seemed to Adrienne to look utterly ravishing in a semi-transparent gown of sea-green gauze. The soft folds of the gown revealed every line of the Comtesse's perfect body, and the seductive lilt of her husky laughter floated back to Adrienne's ears, deafening her to the remarks of her companions, and paralysing her capacity for rational thought. With every flash of sea-green, caught from the corner of her eye, Adrienne felt slightly dowdier and slightly less desirable as the Viscount's bride. She was glad when her mother spoke to her sharply enough to break her out of her dejected reverie.

"La, child, whatever is the matter with you? The dear Viscount has asked you twice if you would care for some refreshment. He has been so kind as to suggest he would fetch us a cool drink while your brother escorts us out on to the balcony. It's such a hot night, I believe Lady Bennett-Smythe has set some tables outside."

"Oh, yes … I mean, no. No, thank you. I don't care for anything just at present." With her extraordinary sensitivity to the Comtesse de la Ronde's movements, Adrienne had already seen the secret glance that flashed between the Viscount and his mistress. With a sickening lurch of her heart, she saw the Comtesse start a leisurely progress towards the dining-salon, which contained the trays and tables of refreshments.

Lady Abbott tapped her daughter's hand teasingly with a fan. "You don't seem to be able to make up your mind to anything today, my love! How fortunate that you will soon have a man to make all your decisions for you!"

Adrienne managed a feeble smile and the Viscount raised her hand to his lips in what must have looked like a tender parting embrace. "Stay with your brother," he ordered coolly, without a trace of tenderness in his voice. "Lady Abbott, I shall return with your ratafia as quickly as possible. Pray don't allow your children to hide you away in a dark corner of the veranda, or I may never find you again."

He strode purposefully towards the door, in the wake of the Comtesse, and Adrienne felt the anger blossoming slowly inside her. She was scarcely aware of her brother's voice, and she followed his courteous suggestion that they move out on to the veranda with the movements of a sleepwalker.

She scarcely waited for her mother to be seated before she spoke breathlessly. "I believe that I am very thirsty, Mama. I shall go and find the Viscount and ask him to bring me some lemonade."

"Let me go for you, Addy."

She detected a note of anxiety in her brother's suggestion, which merely made her more determined than ever to pursue the Viscount. "No, thank you, Peter," she said. "It will be no trouble to go myself."

With a strained smile she walked away, ignoring her mother's agitated demeanour. She bit her lip in an effort to control her tumultuous emotions. She could not – or would not – understand just why she felt so hurt by the Viscount's secret assignation. Mama had told her that it was the duty of a good wife to look the other way in such matters. In the Viscount's case, he had never professed to love her, so it was unrealistic to expect him to pretend any sort of faithfulness.

None of this excellent reasoning had the slightest effect on her simmering emotions, but the bubble of her anger was quickly pierced when she arrived in the dining-salon and found no sign of either the Comtesse or the Viscount. Instead, Mr Bagley, a new puce satin waistcoat gleaming dully in the candlelight, was holding court in front of the lemonade-tray. He caught sight of Adrienne and paused in mid-peroration. She had no difficulty in guessing what he planned to do. He was without doubt about to indulge in a long, jocular and embarrassing burst of congratulations. She looked round for a means of escape and spotted a small embrasure which might afford protection. Dodging nimbly behind a cluster of guests, she escaped from Mr Bagley's line of sight before he could excuse himself from the group of people surrounding him. The embrasure, she saw with relief, was dark and curtained and would keep her out of Mr Bagley's way. She slipped behind the heavy folds of embroidered damask.

The hiding-place did not offer her the haven she had sought. She slipped through the curtains, only to find herself in a small room, lined with books and lit by a single candle. The Viscount, his back turned towards her, was locked in an embrace with the Comtesse de la Ronde. The Comtesse, her hands twined lovingly around the Viscount's neck and her fingers resting in his hair, was pressed tightly against the full length of his body.

Adrienne tried to move, but to her dismay she found that she was immobilised by shock, unable to tear her gaze from the startling tableau in front of her. Heavens, she thought, however does the Comtesse stop her dress from crushing? She had to stuff her hand into her mouth to prevent an hysterical giggle, or perhaps it was a sob, from erupting. It had never occurred to her that people could kiss one another for so long. How do they breathe, she wondered?

She was sufficiently rational to realise that the silly, silent, questions masked a hurt too painful to be examined, and she also knew that it was essential to squeeze back through the curtains before her presence was discovered. But her legs seemed rooted to the ground, as incapable of movement as if they had indeed been planted into the flowering Turkish carpet.

It required a great physical effort to make a move, and in the end her shaky legs betrayed her. She knocked against the narrow opening, causing a rustle of the damask curtains that sounded as loud as a rushing stream in the confines of the silent little room. Both the Viscount and the Comtesse turned towards the hidden entrance.

Adrienne was caught ignominiously in the damask folds with no possibility of retreat. She stared back at the Viscount, unable to think of anything to say, shamed beyond speech by her ludicrous position.

"Did you wish to see me?" the Viscount asked coldly. "I assume you have a good reason for following me." If she had been more experienced, she would have realised that his coldness masked an embarrassment that was at least as great as her own.

"N-no. Y-yes. That is to say, Mama is waiting for her ratafia. And I wished for some lemonade." She tried not to look at the Comtesse de la Ronde, but her eyes were drawn irresistibly towards the slash of sea-green silk. Even in the light of a single candle it seemed that the Comtesse's hair gleamed with the blue-black brilliance of polished ebony. The Comtesse turned her back towards the Viscount and Adrienne, and it was impossible to guess at the state of her feelings.

"If you will return to the dining-salon," the Viscount said, "I shall rejoin you."

She was so glad to get away from the oppressive room, that she almost ran through the curtains, pausing outside to rest her trembling legs against the cool firmness of the plaster wall. She closed her eyes for a minute, and the image of the Comtesse's body, crushed within the Viscount's arms, immediately came into her mind. She shivered with a curious fascination. What would it be like to feel the Viscount's arms wrapped around one's body, and to watch his hard, angry mouth soften into passion?

She thrust the image aside, frightened by the powerful effect it had upon her. Wives, surely, never entertained such thoughts. She forced herself to walk sedately back in the direction of the dining-tables. Mr Bagley was still there and she actually greeted him with a sensation of relief. At least she knew exactly what she felt and thought about Mr Bagley.

The Comtesse was far too clever to move back into the Viscount's arms. She had achieved her purpose by making sure that the silly English virgin witnessed that long, passionate embrace. "She is pretty, your little English bride, *mon amour*," she said as soon as the curtains closed behind Adrienne.

He deliberately ignored her comment. "Why did you drag me in here, Marie-Rose? Much as I relish your expert kisses, you do not normally shower them upon me at a public party. I assume there was some special purpose to your unexpected display of passion?"

She conquered her anger, determined not to reveal her jealousy, and smiled with apparent ease. "I have to leave London for a few days, and I wanted to be sure you would come and visit me again when I return. I do not wish to see you become too full of the domestic virtues, *mon cher*." She risked a brief caress of his cheek, and whispered huskily, "I cannot bear to lose so excellent a lover."

"There is no reason why you should," he said politely, and raised her hand to his lips with the same courteous gesture that had thrilled her many times in the past. "But I shall be busy for several weeks, Marie-Rose. Cravensleigh will be requiring my attention for some time and then it's possible that I may go to Austria."

Even though he spoke gently, she saw that he was not prepared to discuss his wife or his domestic future. She felt a surge of bitterness at this typical English hypocrisy. Whatever the physical intimacy between them, she was merely the Viscount's mistress and therefore not permitted to speak his wife's name.

"What will you be doing in Austria?" she asked, as much for something to say as from a real desire to hear the answer.

"Discovering all Napoleon's secret plans," he said lightly and she couldn't be sure whether or not he was teasing. He dropped another kiss on her fingertips. "*Au revoir*, Marie-Rose." He was gone before she had a chance to utter another word.

When she was alone, the Comtesse smoothed the folds of her gown and adjusted her coiffure with expert fingers. She lifted her shoulders in an affected shrug which disguised her deep and secret sensation of loss. Lady Bennett-Smythe's guests would not be given the chance to crow over her reduced status in the Viscount's life. She returned to the main drawing-room, decked out in her most dazzling smiles and her most brilliant wit. But beneath the glittering exterior, a wound that Viscount Cravensleigh had never intended to inflict was opened in the Comtesse's heart and began to fester.

CHAPTER
EIGHT

The wedding of Miss Adrienne Abbott to Viscount
Cravensleigh was universally proclaimed the event of
the year. The fact that it occurred almost three weeks
after the end of the Season scarcely detracted from its
lustre. The news that Sir Arthur Wellesley was
marching his army from Portugal into Spain, even as
Adrienne Abbott was becoming the Fifth Viscountess
Cravensleigh, certainly offered no competition. The
manoeuvrings of the largest land army England had
ever sent overseas did not, as far as Society was
concerned, constitute an Event.

During the period of her brief betrothal, Miss
Abbott's gowns, behaviour, antecedents and prospects
had all been exhaustively discussed and pronounced
acceptable. Society was gratified to observe that this
approval was not misplaced, for on her wedding day
the bride seemed overwhelmed by the good fortune
that had come her way. She trembled visibly during
the ceremony and looked paler, more ethereal and
more beautiful than she usually did. The Viscount, of
course, merely looked handsome and cynical, which
was only to be expected since he was a man and men
were never much fun at weddings.

Lady Abbott wept copious tears and Sir George
tried hard not to appear overly pleased with himself.

Society acknowledged that he had cause for self-congratulation. Not every baronet, not even one as comfortably placed as Sir George, could hope to see his elder daughter married to a baron and his younger daughter to a viscount within the space of two seasons. All in all, Society decided, the wedding marked a highly successful conclusion to the activities of the season.

Apart from the Comtesse de la Ronde, only two people failed to share in the general satisfaction and they, unfortunately were the bridal couple. Adrienne had endured the three long weeks before the wedding ceremony in a spirit of numb resignation. It seemed to her that all hope of making friends with the Viscount had been dissipated after Lady Bennett-Smythe's disastrous party.

As for the Viscount, at one moment he felt tantalised by the distant reserve of Adrienne's manner and wished he could break through the cool surface to the passionate emotions he was certain lay beneath. At the next moment he felt nothing but fury at the way his life had been arranged for him and wondered if even the estate of Cravensleigh was worth the acquisition of an unwilling wife.

They were both white from a mixture of physical and emotional exhaustion when they finally found themselves alone in the private sitting-room of the Viscount's town house. Their journey to Cravensleigh Manor was due to start early the following morning, and so they faced up to the necessity of an evening spent in one another's company. Denby placed a bottle of burgundy within reach of his master's arm, and a jug of freshly squeezed lemonade beside the Viscountess.

"Would you care for something to eat, my lady?"

Adrienne didn't answer for a minute and then realised that she was "my lady". "Oh," she said, startled to think of herself as this newly important personage. "No, thank you, Denby."

"My lord, is there anything I can get you?"

"No. You can clear off, Denby. I shan't be needing you again tonight."

Denby bowed, hesitated on the brink of speech, and then decided to withdraw to the cavernous reaches of the basement kitchens in a judicious silence. It was left to the Viscount to find something to say, since Adrienne was frozen into speechlessness.

"To your health, my dear," he said as he raised a brimming tumbler. "Allow me to offer you my felicitations. You have carried off your first performance as my Viscountess with a touch of genius. My friends won't stop congratulating me on my good fortune for a twelve-month."

She was too tired to parry his subtle taunts with any subtleties of her own. "My lord," she said wearily. "We are married now, for good or ill. We have to spend our lives together. Shall we not try to make the best of it? Even if we are not likely to meet one another very often, it would surely be more comfortable if we could be friends!"

"Friends!" The idea of a husband and wife who were both friends and comfortable in one another's company was so novel that the Viscount's mockery was stopped almost before it had begun. "I find it a little difficult to offer you my friendship, madam," he said curtly. "Our past relationship has not been conducive to the development of mutual understanding."

She sank down on to the sofa, aware of the fact that her shoulders drooped listlessly, but unable to jerk herself upright. "This is supposed to be a marriage of convenience, but surely it isn't going to be very convenient if we are condemned to dislike one another almost before our lives together have begun?"

"What foundation do we have for a friendship?" the Viscount asked. "What interests do we share? How can a man be *friendly* towards a woman?" Deliberately he thrust aside the memory of their first few meetings, when they had seemed able to talk and laugh together with a special sort of intimacy.

"Your wish to regain the estate of Cravensleigh was the cause of our marriage," said Adrienne. "And it is where I shall have to make my home. Don't you think we might find common interests in Cravensleigh during the next few weeks when you have said we must stay together in the country?"

He did not want to respond to the soft appeal he could see in her eyes. He recognised instinctively that friendship with his wife would draw him back into the world of emotions he had put aside more than ten years before, when his first love had been taken from him. He forced himself to speak with a deliberate sneer. "So you have already assigned my role to me, I see. You expect me to play the part of a dutiful country squire, while you play the role of the virtuous country housewife."

"I don't expect you to do anything," she said and the Viscount could hear her voice crack slightly on the final word. He saw that she swallowed hard, as if determined to ensure that no tears would emerge. "If you would prefer never to see me, my lord, I can just as easily arrange to keep out of your way."

He was touched by her silent misery, then angry with himself for allowing a woman to play upon his emotions once again. He had no wish to lay his innermost feelings at the feet of this slip of a girl. He refilled his glass and goaded himself to speak to her with casual insolence. "My dear, I cannot allow you to escape your wifely duties so easily. Naturally, I shall have to see you. Pleasant as I should find it to pretend that you don't exist, you surely can't have forgotten that we have to provide the estate with an heir? Your mother is such a firm believer in the institution of marriage that I can't imagine she failed to warn you of your duty to provide me with a son."

She shivered at the deliberately insulting tone. "But not yet? Please, my lord ... Not just yet."

"You flatter yourself, my dear, if you imagine I feel any impatience to fulfill my obligations to the estate." Angrily he crashed his glass down on the table. "Oh, don't worry, madam, it will not be yet. Summon your maid and go to bed. Leave me to enjoy myself in my accustomed fashion."

A footman answered her hasty tug of the bellrope, already bearing a branch of flaming candles to light the way to her bedroom. She started to leave the room then paused uncertainly in the doorway. "Goodnight, my lord. I trust ... I trust you will sleep well."

Her voice was so shaky that he bit back the retort that sprang to his lips. He raised his wineglass to her in a mocking salutation. "You see that I have an infallible aid to untroubled slumber. Please see that your maid has you ready to leave Cravensleigh at dawn."

The Cravensleigh lands lay in the heart of Warwickshire, a county previously unknown to Adrienne. The estate was almost a hundred miles distant from London and there was no possibility of accomplishing the journey in a single day, a circumstance that appeared to annoy the Viscount much more than Adrienne.

She did not mind the endless hours in the carriage. It was well sprung, with large, clear-glass windows and she soon became accustomed to the swaying of the coach: a motion which was familiar to her after two long journeys from Abbott's Grange to London. The day was sunny, but cooled by a persistent breeze and she took pleasure in observing the changing scene outside her window. The brick cottages of Harrow shortly gave way to the familiar timber and plaster of the Buckinghamshire villages. The English country-side was very beautiful, she thought, and in summer, at least, the villagers she saw through the carriage windows looked healthy and well fed.

Since the Viscount chose to ride his own horse, she was spared any necessity of finding topics of conversation to share with her new husband, a state of affairs that no doubt pleased him as much as it did her. Sally, her new maid, was seated across from her in the coach, and although she responded politely whenever Adrienne spoke to her, she naturally never introduced any conversation. It was the maid's first journey outside London and she spent much of the journey with her nose pressed against the carriage window, a permanent frown of amazement wrinkled between her eyebrows.

They spent the night at an excellent posting-inn which had been notified by Denby of their impending arrival. The innkeeper and his wife spared no effort to ensure that their noble patrons were well catered for, and the maid proved that, although she was unused to country inns and country animals (she confessed that she had not thought there were so many sheep in the entire world as they had seen during the course of the day's travelling), her skills as a personal servant were of the highest order.

Between bathing away the dust from the road and consuming a substantial dinner, the hours after sunset were filled. Adrienne and the Viscount were able to retire to their separate chambers having exchanged scarcely more than twenty sentences during the entire course of the day.

The second day promised them as fair a journey as the first. The countryside, although sparsely populated in some parts, showed signs of great fertility and the ground was lush with ripening wheat and orchards of laden apple trees. Adrienne's mood, so strained since the announcement of her betrothal, began to lighten. It was impossible to feel that life held out no prospect of enjoyment when the fields gleamed with pale golden richness and the butterflies danced against the windows of the carriage. She happened to catch the maid's eye and she smiled. Sally smiled back.

I am happy, Adrienne thought with a sudden sense of wonder. I am married. I have my own home. I'm going to Cravensleigh, which is *my* home. Who knows what may happen at Cravensleigh? Perhaps the Viscount will even learn to love me.

The thought popped unbidden into her mind, piercing the glow of content. Adrienne thrust the thought aside. What did it matter whether or not the Viscount loved her? Equally unbidden came the unwelcome answer. It mattered because, despite all the good reasons why she should not, she had fallen in love with her husband.

The realisation was at first too surprising to leave room for other emotions, but once she had accepted the truth, Adrienne felt misery gnawing at the edges of her previous happiness. The prospect of living for years under the lash of the Viscount's indifference was more than she could tolerate.

After a few miles of mournfulness, however, Adrienne's spirits began to rise. The sun was still shining, the fields were still promising a bountiful harvest and the butterflies still flew around her carriage. She reminded herself that she was young, a Beauty (if the Prince of Wales could be believed), and she was supposed to be clever. She was not altogether certain that this last quality was an aid to her cause, but despite Mama's oft-expressed views to the contrary, Adrienne couldn't help thinking that in devising methods to make the Viscount fall in love with her, cleverness must be of some use.

She had reached this optimistic point in her ruminations when the carriage drew to a halt beside a small wayside inn. The Viscount, already dismounted, came to the coach and unlocked the door so that she and the maid could descend.

"We are nearing Cravensleigh," he said. "Two hours of driving – a little more – will carry us on to my land."

There was no mistaking the throb of mingled pleasure and pride which warmed his words. She wondered again at the reckless mood of desperate boredom which must have caused him to stake something so precious on the turn of a few cards. She resolved that, if she could help it, he would never again sink to such a level of desperation. "I am looking forward to our arrival," she said truthfully. "I hope … I think we shall be very happy at Cravensleigh."

Some of the fervour of her silent hopes must have shone through the simple words, for he looked at her closely although in the end he said nothing. He offered his hands to assist her down the carriage steps. "I thought you would like to take some air," he said. "It must be tedious for you to sit so long in the carriage."

"No," she said. "I have enjoyed seeing so much countryside which is new to me. We have been fortunate to have such perfect weather for our journey."

"Yes," he smiled. "The heavens have been on our side."

He appeared to regret his moment of friendliness, for he gestured curtly to a wooden table placed beneath the branches of an oak tree. Pillows had already been brought out to cover the simple wooden benches and the innkeeper and his wife were bowing low in welcome.

"Please be seated, madam," said the Viscount. "The innkeeper here has nothing but cider and bread and cheese to offer us, but I think you will find it all of excellent quality."

Adrienne was glad to have a respite from the rocking of the coach. It was cool beneath the leafy branches of the oak, and the cider foamed with a tart freshness in the pewter tumbler.

The Viscount was well known at the inn and was quickly involved in a conversation that was divided equally between the favourable prospects for this year's harvest and the worms which had blighted last year's crop of apples. The worms, the innkeeper informed them, had been shipped in by Napoleon especially to plague the honest farmers of Warwick. He didn't speculate upon the French government's method of transporting the worms from the coast over almost a hundred miles of hostile English countryside to Warwick. The malevolent cunning of all Frenchmen was an agreed fact of life.

Adrienne listened to the innkeeper with only part of her attention, for the cider made her pleasantly sleepy. Her maid, however, had edged closer to the group of men and was listening intently to the flow of the discussion. Her forehead was creased with wrinkles of concentration and her mouth hung slightly open, so deep was her absorption. It was difficult to recognise the supercilious maid her mother had hired in this eager and gawping girl. Adrienne realised that the thick, rolling accents of Warwickshire must be as fascinating and almost as incomprehensible to her London-bred maid as a foreign language.

In the distance, Adrienne heard the familiar sounds of fresh horses being led out from the shed which served as the inn's stable, but it seemed too much of an effort to twist her head round and watch the progress of the grooms. Instead, she relaxed against the rough bark of the tree-trunk and gave a sigh of contentment.

"It's very peaceful here," she murmured to the world at large.

"But if you don't mind, we had better move on before you fall completely asleep." The Viscount's voice had lost its haughtiness, and sounded almost amused. "I should have warned you about the strength of Jackson's cider. Allow me to offer you my arm."

She smiled at him, some of her shyness vanquished by the alcohol. Her cheeks were flushed by the touch of the sun and her thick lashes drooped a little sleepily over her eyes.

"I like Warwickshire," she said.

"Especially Mrs Jackson's cider!" This time there was no mistaking the laughter in his voice. He helped her carefully into the carriage. "Not much further now, and you will be able to rest properly. I sent

Denby on ahead to Cravensleigh. He will let them know that we are arriving and he will also make sure that you are not expected to greet a regiment of family retainers as soon as we arrive."

She was grateful for his thoughtfulness, and smiled at him again. "Thank you," she whispered. "I shall try to be the wife you wish for, my lord."

He drew back as she spoke, perhaps only to let the maid enter, but her mood of sleepy contentment was interrupted. He shut the door behind the maid and sprang on to his own chestnut gelding, which was being held by an elderly ostler. "We will stop at the boundary of my land and ride up to the house together, in the carriage." He pulled on his leather riding-gauntlets and was gone.

Her sleepiness vanished completely with his departure. She leaned forward on to the edge of the seat, filled with a strange restlessness that prevented her taking any enjoyment in observing the land that surrounded her husband's estates. The roads had been deteriorating in calibre ever since they entered Warwickshire, and their rutted surface was now made even more hazardous by deep potholes. She glanced at her maid, and saw that she had finally dozed off, despite the turbulent rocking of the coach over the rough roads.

Her casual glance saved the maid's life. The carriage swayed into a particularly deep hole at the same moment as a single gunshot rang out in the stillness of the warm afternoon. One of the horses, frisky from the plentiful oats provided by innkeeper Jackson, reared in the traces of the carriage then tried to bolt. The coachwheel, jammed in a large pothole, tore off its axle and the cumbersome travelling-coach sank to the ground in a splinter of torn wood and broken iron. Inside the carriage, the largest of the brass lanterns was jerked off its moorings as the carriage collapsed on its side.

Even as she felt herself hurled against the padded door of the coach, Adrienne saw that her maid's head was in direct line of the falling lamp and she launched herself towards the opposite seat, thrusting the maid's head from its appointment with disaster. Instead, her own shoulder received the full force of the lantern's blow. She heard only a brief, muffled groan from Sally, an agitated cry from the groom and then a swift string of shouted commands from the Viscount before the pain of her injury precipitated her into merciful darkness.

CHAPTER
NINE

A fresh breeze rippled across Adrienne's face, and she struggled to sit upright. She felt a patch of rough gravel move beneath her, and she wondered vaguely why she was no longer inside the coach. It was too much effort to think or to move, and she collapsed back in to the arms waiting to receive her. She was lying, she realised suddenly, with her head cushioned against the Viscount's chest and her body supported against his arm. His hands were caressing her body with unbelievable tenderness.

Her lashes flickered wide open in astonishment and for a moment her eyes were locked into the cool depths of his. The Viscount's hands immediately paused in their task and, with the return of full consciousness, she understood that he had not been caressing her, but searching gently for the source and extent of her injuries.

"My shoulder …" she whispered, and then shut her eyes to blot out the pain. Not the physical pain, but the mental pain that came from the knowledge that the gentleness of his embrace had only been a figment of her fevered imagination.

"Sally … my maid … What happened to her?" she asked.

"Hush, you must not disturb yourself. The maid is perfectly well. She told us what happened and, thanks to your prompt action, she is in far better case than you. Except for the fact that she is showing an alarming tendency to go off into strong hysterics." His fingers probed once again at the agony of her shoulder and she could not hold back a gasp of anguish.

His voice was kindly but cool when he spoke again. This was probably the voice he reserved for soothing his most valuable horses, she thought, wishing she could emulate her maid and succumb to hysterics. She conquered the urge. "What did you say?" she murmured, when she realised that the Viscount was speaking.

He repeated his question patiently. "Do you think you will be able to bear the pain of riding in front of me back to the inn? We can then send for another carriage and for the services of my own physician. I don't believe there has been any dislocation of your shoulder, or any broken bones, and it would be safe -- though uncomfortable – to ride with me."

She nodded her head, because the effort of speaking seemed temporarily beyond the power of her resources. "Good girl!" he said. "You are certainly showing the Cravensleigh spirit."He raised his voice only slightly, but there was no mistaking the urgency of his command. "Joshua! Tom! Come here and support the Viscountess while I mount."

She saw that there was blood on his riding-jacket and she wondered how he had wounded himself until she realised that the blood came from the deep gash in her own shoulder. The two servants knelt down beside her on the roadside. With clumsy but willing hands they cushioned her aching body in their arms. Through a haze of pain she saw the Viscount mount upon his chestnut gelding, and the servants immediately made respectful efforts to assist her to her feet. They would not allow her to walk, but carried her close to the side of the chestnut gelding and, while a groom held the horse's head, the Viscount reached down to clasp her waist. In one swift moment of excruciating pain he lifted her up and seated her in front of him.

"Lean against me," he said curtly, but the order wasn't necessary, for the throbbing of her shoulder made all attempts at decorum or pride equally impossible. "I shall keep the horse to a walk," he said. "It's less than three miles back to the inn, so we should be there within half an hour."

She couldn't answer him. It required all her attention to remain more or less upright on the horse. The pain of her shoulder was sufficient to block out all minor discomfort and all awareness of their progress along the winding country road, but it wasn't quite enough to overcome the tingling sensations along her spine, wherever her back came into contact with the Viscount's body. His arms enfolded her within the security of his embrace and he maintained a flow of comforting conversation which required no response from her.

It seemed half a lifetime later when she saw the inn through a shimmering mist of fading consciousness. The innkeeper and his wife moved through the edges of her pain like concerned but insubstantial shadows. Only the blood seeping from her shoulder and the touch of the Viscount's hands seemed real. He lifted her into Mr Jackson's outstretched arms – like a dying calf, she thought with a silent, hysterical laugh – and then sprang swiftly from the saddle. He tossed the reins into Mrs Jackson's grasp, indifferent to the fact that the poor woman had probably never before controlled a carthorse, let alone a hundred guineas'-

worth of thoroughbred flesh.

"I will carry the Viscountess," he said. His voice sounded almost angry, Adrienne thought dreamily, too far removed from reality to worry about the cause of his anger.

"I don't think I can walk ... It hurts ..." she said, dreading the prospect of climbing stairs in search of the bedchamber.

"There is no need for you to walk," the Viscount replied, and his voice was calm once again. "Jackson will bring pillows and covers to the settle in the taproom. You will be quite comfortable. I shall see to it."

"Yes," she said, allowing her lashes to close over her eyes. "You will see to it."

She was woken by the sound of rain, drumming against the casements in an unceasing patter. She didn't want to open her eyes. It was warm and safe in the bed, and she felt isolated from all her previous problems. She stirred against the comfort of several soft white pillows and forced her eyes open, glad that the intensity of pain had at last diminished. A cool hand touched her forehead and she turned round to look more closely at the Viscount, who was standing by her bedside.

"I see you have at last deigned to return to my company," he said, and she could sense the relief behind his words. "We began to wonder if you had deserted us permanently."

She struggled to sit upright. "I am in bed, not on the settle," she murmured. She saw the clean white nightgown she was wearing. "My clothes ... What time is it?"

"You had better ask what day," replied the Viscount. "It's Saturday morning."

"Saturday! But it was Thursday!" She found it hard to formulate her thoughts in longer sentences.

"Indeed it was. You have kept us all in a fine state of suspense, I can assure you. It's hard to know who has been more apologetic. Your maid blames herself for falling asleep in the coach. The postilions say they should never have allowed the coach to fall into so deep a rut. The farmer came and apologised for shooting at rabbits. I dare say even the horses are feeling guilty because they dared to kick over their traces. I have had my work cut out keeping all the penitents from your door, believe me."

"Even the horses?" she asked, and winced when an unwary movement reminded her of the cuts and bruises covering her shoulder.

He gave a crack of laughter. "Well, now I know you are beginning to recover! The lamp inflicted a jagged cut and severe bruises around your shoulder and back. The doctor told us the wound had become infected and you were delirious for quite a while."

She wondered just what she might have revealed during her delirium, but the Viscount was smiling at her quite calmly, so she decided she couldn't have babbled about her feelings for him.

"Anyway," said the Viscount cheerfully, "that is all over now and the wound is beginning to heal just as it should. I will send in your maid with some breakfast, but you will have to spend today in bed."

She was too weak to protest these authoritative orders, although she chafed under her own helplessness. "What about your journey to Cravensleigh, my lord? You must be very annoyed at the delay."

"Cravensleigh has not seen me for six months," he said. "It may wait for another few days until you are well. A different travelling carriage has been sent for, and when you feel fit enough, we will carry on with our journey. There is no rush."

It was two days before the interrupted journey to Cravensleigh was finally completed. They set out early on a fine summer morning, in a coach padded almost to the roof with cushions. The interior lanterns had been removed and Sally, the maid, was banished to a gig. The Viscount himself assisted Adrienne into the carriage, and remained by her side for the short journey.

"I cannot risk you bruising the other shoulder," he told her. "Otherwise we shall be celebrating our first wedding anniversary without ever having left the boundary of old Jackson's inn."

She laughed and tried not to pay too much attention to the warm light that turned the Viscount's eyes from chilly grey to affectionate blue. If her heart was beating too fast, nobody should guess it. "I think you are just jealous of my opportunity to play the heroine," she said lightly. "For shame, my lord, and Sally was convinced she had joined the service of a truly noble mistress!"

The jolting of the carriage troubled her more than she cared to admit, for the wound was not healed and she felt that it threatened to open with every jerk of the carriage. The Viscount seemed unaware of her discomfort and talked determinedly of his neighbours, their land and their foibles, so that she was forced to make some effort to reply. Only when the carriage finally moved on to the gravelled smoothness of the drive up to Cravensleigh itself, did the Viscount's flow of chatter cease.

"Let me see your shoulder." Gently, but firmly, he caused her to lean forward. "Thank God!" he said when he had pushed back her jacket and examined the fine beige wool of her travelling-dress. "There is no blood, so the wound must have remained closed." He smiled at her. "You have been thinking me a monster of inhumanity, I know. But it was better to keep your mind off your shoulder, if I possibly could." He leaned out of the coach window and called to the postilions. "Halt the horses at the crest of the rise. I wish to show her ladyship the house."

The early sun had disappeared and a fine mist of summer rain was falling when the driver halted the coach at the top of a small hill. Cravensleigh Manor was stretched out before Adrienne's eyes.

The name should have given her a clue of what to expect, even though the estate land was so extensive. In her mind, she had built up the image of an imposing stone residence, much decorated with tall columns and coloured marble. The reality was rather different. Cravensleigh was a low, rambling manor house, dating from the Elizabethan period and built of mellowed pink brick. Some Cravensleigh ancestor, anxious to flatter his monarch, had shaped the house in the form of a letter E, and the three wings enclosed spacious courtyards, edged with banks of marigolds, hollyhocks and snapdragons.

The faded pink brick of the many chimneys gleamed through the silver greyness of the light rain, and Adrienne felt her heart contract with a sharp pleasure that bordered on pain. It would be so easy – far too easy – to fall in love with this welcoming mansion.

"It's beautiful," she said. "The brick glistens in the rain, like a flower."

"Yes," said the Viscount. "Cravensleigh is beautiful." His eyes narrowed as he stared at the house through the thin veil of rain. "I was a fool to risk losing it."

As if he was conscious of revealing more than he had intended, he lifted up the glass window with a snap of the strap. "You will get wet if you lean out to look at the house," he said. He called out sharply to the servants. "Drive on! Her ladyship must rest."

The idyllic summer days slipped by, changing into weeks almost before Adrienne was aware of it. It seemed that the accident had altered her relationship with the Viscount, and although they were still wary of one another, there was no longer any hostility between them. Friendship and a hesitant mutual respect started to replace the bitterness.

The cuts on her shoulder soon healed, and the virulent purple bruises faded, although a lingering stiffness hampered her movements. A few of the neighbours started to call, and she accepted their tentative gestures of sociability. She kept reminding herself that when the Viscount returned to London, as he must soon do, she would need all the local friends she could possibly manage to find in order to fill the emptiness of her days.

The Viscount ignored his originally stated plan of avoiding the company of his wife, and they spent the major portion of each day together, separating only after dinner at night or when urgent estate business called the Viscount away. Contrary to Adrienne's expectations, the staff at Cravensleigh didn't resent her presence. The housekeeper and the cook were both young women and they performed their tasks with quiet, respectful efficiency, showing no signs of mourning the days of the Viscount's bachelorhood. They seemed to welcome the few suggestions and orders which were all Adrienne considered necessary to ensure the smooth running of the household.

The cook, a thin woman who surely never tasted her own magnificent confections, would have been despised in a London kitchen. She prepared simple, traditional country meals: pies, roasted game-birds, jugged hare. She made use of the fresh fruits and vegetables that abounded on the estate, and knew little of the elaborate sauces and heavy spices that formed the basis of fashionable London cuisine.

The Viscount looked up one evening from a satisfying over-indulgence in gooseberry pie, smothered in thick clots of cream from Cravensleigh cows and found his wife's eyes fixed upon him with a decided twinkle.

"It is very good pie," he said defensively.

"Certainly it is," she said. "I knew it must be one of your *special* favourites when you helped yourself to a third portion."

He laughed ruefully. "I had forgotten how good it is to know exactly what one is eating. Sometimes I wonder what is actually lurking underneath all that aspic and nutmeg on the London tables."

She laughed in turn. "You had better not let Alphonse hear you uttering such blasphemies!"

"Who is Alphonse?"

She looked at him steadily before replying. "Alphonse is your chef in London."

"Ah!" The Viscount fiddled with the narrow stem of his crystal wine goblet. "How did you come to meet him? You were in London with me for only one night."

She lifted her shoulders in a tiny shrug, not wanting to appear as though she had intruded so quickly on the organisation of one of his houses. "I saw that somebody had prepared a very elaborate breakfast for us on the day we left town. You may have noticed the exquisite iced fruit sorbet? I just slipped in to the kitchens to offer the chef our thanks."

"I see." He did not pursue the subject. "Perhaps you would walk·upstairs with me before I am tempted to indulge in a fourth helping of this gooseberry pie? Not as exquisite as Alphonse's ice sculptures, perhaps, but certainly excellent of its kind."

By the end of the second week she was able to ride a pony-trap without any discomfort and the Viscount started to escort her personally to every corner of his estate. Adrienne enjoyed meeting his tenant-farmers, and was pleased to see that even the labourers were housed well in sturdy stone cottages that had wooden floors and usually an upstairs loft where the family could sleep. She discovered that it was the Viscount's custom to give each newly wed couple a bed, so that hard-earned money could be saved for tables, chairs and sometimes for the luxury of a cast-iron oven to be installed alongside the fire-grate. Adrienne had been accustomed from childhood to seeing healthy labourers working in her father's fields, and sturdy children at their mother's heels during the haymaking. Nevertheless, the comfort of these Cravensleigh cottages was new to her.

"Your estate shows no signs of neglect, my lord," she said one day to the Viscount. "Even though you haven't been here for six months, your people seem prosperous. No greedy land-agent has been allowing roofs to leak and floors to rot!"

"Did you expect to find that I had ground the faces of the poor into the dust of the land in order to pay for my addiction to the gaming-tables?" There was a trace of bitterness in the Viscount's voice. He shrugged. "Besides, you are forgetting that my father has been supervising the estate recently. His authority, believe me, is not lightly flouted. Not even by greedy land-agents or errant sons.''

She deliberately ignored the final thrust. "Your father cannot be responsible for all the signs of prosperity. Cravensleigh has obviously been well cared for over a period of several years.''

"Baggott is an excellent agent," said the Viscount.

She saw that he would claim no personal credit for the sound management of his estate. "Baggott is to be congratulated," she said. "But do you feel there is no room for improvement upon his methods?''

"There is always room for improvement in farming," he said. "We haven't taken advantage of advances in other parts of England. The soil in Warwickshire is naturally fertile and I have been too self-absorbed in the past to care about increasing the yield of the land." He frowned, then added, "But I am planning to change all that, and I shall have to spend more time here than I thought at first. It will take some months to persuade all the labourers of the advantages that will come from using new methods.''

Her pulses leaped a little at his words, but she managed to say jokingly, "You will have your work cut out for you if you start *anything* new! My father tried to persuade his tenant-farmers to dig irrigation ditches and fence off part of their fields to protect the grazing. From the objections his tenants made, you would have thought he had recommended planting a rotating crop of poison!''

He started to smile, then turned away abruptly. "You are very clever, are you not?" he said suddenly. "You have achieved just what you set out to achieve. Beguiling me with your beauty, prodding me on with your interest and your suggestions about Cravensleigh.''

"My lord? I don't understand what you mean.''

"Do you not? You even told me that you would do it. You warned me on the day that we married that you would forge Cravensleigh into a bond between us." He laughed, but without mirth. "And here I am! The devoted country squire, jogging around the countryside in a pony-cart, with my wife at my side!"

She looked away from him, hurt by the sarcasm of his words.

"I didn't set out to be ... beguiling ... my lord. I am sorry if you have found my interest in Cravensleigh offensive." Her breath caught slightly in her throat. "It is surely quite a natural interest. After all, you have told me Cravensleigh is to be my permanent home. You will be travelling, but I shall always be here."

"Are you hoping to make me feel guilty?" he asked, and then with a change of mood Adrienne found incomprehensible, he turned to her and spoke in a low, husky murmur. "No, no! It will not do. Adrienne, if only you knew what you are doing to me ..." He drew a deep breath and said more calmly. "I don't resent your interest in Cravensleigh. I'm glad that you find so much to interest you in my estate."

She was anxious to respond to his renewed friendship and she spoke eagerly. "I have noticed that several of the older women are very talented with their needles," she said. "How did so many of them learn to knit and sew and even to make lace?"

"My grandmother was an active woman," replied the Viscount, his face softening as if with pleasant memories. "She started a school while she was Viscountess Cravensleigh. She taught the women of the estate simple arithmetic and helped every woman to learn to write her own name and the name of all her children. As soon as they had mastered the alphabet, she started to teach them simple sewing and embroidery. Some of the men actually learned how to knit, since it helped to fill the long, idle days of winter."

"But the young women seem less skilled than their parents," said Adrienne.

He paused a moment before replying. "Yes," he said eventually. "My mother was always more interested in London life than in the affairs of Cravensleigh and she didn't feel able or willing to devote any time to carrying on the tradition. I'm afraid the skills are gradually dying out. A few of the young girls are taught to sew or knit by their grandmothers, but very few of them can write their names or do the simplest of sums."

Adrienne's eyes lit up with excitement. At last she had found something she could do to fill the long, empty months when the Viscount would leave her to return to the pleasures of town. "Oh, that is what I could do!" she exclaimed. "Please say that I may have your permission to start a school for young girls. It is something I should so much like to do!"

The Viscount seemed ominously silent, and she wondered if he sensed an implied rebuke for his mother's negligence in allowing the school to fade away. "We could use whatever building your grandmother used," she said. She tried to curb the enthusiasm that still filled her voice. "I would only teach the girls after the harvest is completed, so they would not neglect their work in the fields. We would use the cheapest of materials. We would only need to provide some hessian so that they could learn their stitches; a few slates and some chalk. Don't you think we could do that, my lord?"

He was silent for so long she believed she had offended him. He finally gave a harsh laugh. "Do you know how much money I wagered the night I lost Cravensleigh? Thirty thousand guineas, my dear, staked on the turn of a single card. And you are begging me for a few shillings to spend on schoolroom supplies!" He stared out across the apple orchard that lined both sides of the narrow drive they were following. "Buy your slates," he said at last. "And anything else you need. You don't have to ask me for permission."

"Thank you, my lord." Her face was flushed with pleasure, her eyes shining. She had already forgotten his earlier flash of temper. In her mind's eye she could picture the schoolroom, its benches filled with children, neatly scrubbed and pinafored. If they could learn to write their names, she thought, why couldn't they learn all the alphabet? Could they even learn to read? Her imagination had already leapt forward to a generation of young girls reading their own Bibles in a Sunday School, and surrounded at home by brightly patterned cushions and curtains of their own design.

"What are you thinking about?" The Viscount looked at her curiously.

"Oh, n-nothing. I was just day-dreaming about the school," she said hurriedly.

"You are the oddest creature," he said. "You go into a positive trance of pleasure at the thought of providing schooling to a collection of yokels who won't thank you for your efforts. I am sure they would rather romp in the hayfields than learn how to set stitches in a sampler."

"Just as you are sure that all women would prefer to twirl round the dance-floor rather than do anything useful," she said before she could stop herself.

"Twirling around the dance-floor, my dear, is supremely useful. That is how a young lady bedazzles a young man into offering her the benefits of matrimony.''

"Not every woman is as anxious for marriage as you insist upon believing,'' Adrienne said with a flash of her old spirit. "It is not the universal panacea for female ills, you know.''

To her surprise the Viscount laughed. "I am not going to oblige you by having a quarrel,'' he said. "I have decided to stop castigating myself for enticing you into marriage. It is quite clear to me that you have lost your heart to Cravensleigh. In fact, I don't think there is anything you could say to convince me that you would prefer to be in London at this moment.''

"No,'' she said after a little pause. "I wouldn't prefer to be in London.''

He pulled the trap to a halt, placing his hand beneath her chin and lifting her face gently until she was forced to look up at him.

"Am I right in thinking you are happier here than you were with your parents at Abbott's Grange?''

She didn't answer and he repeated insistently, "Tell me, Adrienne, are you happy?''

She dropped her lashes quickly to veil the leap of longing in her eyes. "Yes,'' she said. "I like living at Cravensleigh.''

He smiled wryly. "I suppose I deserved that noncommittal answer.'' His eyes seemed fixed upon the soft outlines of her mouth and she bit her lip to prevent it trembling beneath his gaze. "Don't do that!'' he commanded softly, touching his finger to her lips.

She tried to turn away, but he still cupped her face with his hands. "You have made your lip bleed,'' he said. "Shall I kiss it better?''

She tried to laugh, as though she were confident he was only teasing. "Why that is just to comfort children, my lord.''

"But this is not," he said and gathered her into his arms to kiss her.

She could think of nothing to say when he finally released her. None of Mama's warnings had prepared her for the incredible sensations that had ripped through her entire body as the Viscount took her into his arms. She occupied herself in retying the strings of her straw hat, which had fallen back on to her shoulders. She was relieved when the Viscount started to speak.

"It's a good job that Bessie is such a placid horse," he said with rather an odd catch in his voice. "Otherwise I might have had a bolting animal to contend with as well as everything else."

She was dismayed by his words. Evidently he had not been very well pleased by her response to his kiss. She cleared her throat. "I ... er ... I have never ... That is to say, isn't it time for us to return to the house?"

"Yes," said the Viscount with another odd laugh. "I think it is probably well past time."

The maid finished tying the last of the ribbons on her mistress's nightgown. "Your bruises have all gone, my lady," she said with evident satisfaction. "There's still a faint scar from where that pesky lantern hit you, but I dare say it will fade in time."

"I shall just have to drape a gauze scarf about my shoulders," said Adrienne. "Fortunately, it is likely to be some months before I am wearing a ballgown again." She thought wryly that it might, in fact, be years before the Viscount decided to invite her back to London, and she would have no pleasure in going there alone.

"My lady, do you mean ...? Oh, I am so pleased, my lady!"

She looked at the maid in surprise. "What are you talking about, Sally?"

The maid seemed flustered. "I thought perhaps you meant that the Cravensleigh estate was to have an heir, my lady. I am sorry if I spoke out of turn, my lady. I didn't mean no harm."

Adrienne blushed. "You misunderstood my meaning, Sally."

To cover their mutual confusion, the maid picked up a hairbrush and began to administer several unnecessary strokes to Adrienne's already gleaming tresses. "Your hair looks like silk tonight, my lady," she said. "Just like bronze silk."

Adrienne dismissed the words with an easy laugh. "Well, if bronze silk hair should ever happen to become fashionable, I am certainly in luck. Unfortunately, I believe golden ringlets were the rage last year and raven black ringlets this year. That means auburn waves will be all the crack next season. Polished bronze, and dead straight at that, will never make the social scene, I'm afraid."

"Fashion isn't everything," said Sally stubbornly.

"Now I know the Warwickshire air has affected your brain!" exclaimed Adrienne. "I never thought I would hear a lady's maid, trained in London, who would dare to give voice to such a sacrilegious remark! You had better go to bed and get a good night's sleep, before all vestiges of your training desert you!"

Sally giggled. "Very well, my lady." It was hard to believe that this cheerful girl was the same haughty maid who had presented herself for an interview just before Adrienne's marriage. I don't seem to be very good at being dignified with servants, thought

Adrienne as Sally walked bouncily across the room.
She sighed, chalking another failure on to her slate.
She wondered how her mother, so competent in
organising a genteel household, had managed to
produce such an unsatisfactory daughter.

The maid had scarcely closed the door before her
miserable reflections were interrupted by a sharp
knock. "Come in, Sally," she called.

"It is I, not your maid."

She whirled round from her chair in front of the
dressing-table. "My lord? Is something wrong?"

As she spoke, she dropped her eyes into her lap, so
that she would not have to cope with the
overwhelming sight of her husband, clad in a long,
peacock-blue dressing-gown. By a fortunate accident,
she was still holding the hairbrush and she began to
brush her hair very busily, staring into the mirror so
that she wouldn't have to stare at the Viscount.

He walked across the room and quite gently placed
his hands over hers, stilling their agitated movement.
"You look beautiful already," he said. "Don't waste
time trying to improve upon perfection."

She wished that she could dismiss his words as
easily as she had dismissed the maid's similar
compliments. Instead, her breath caught in her throat
and she could feel her heart start to beat with an
erratic, urgent rhythm.

"What do you want, my lord?" she asked again. "I
hope there is nothing wrong?"

He looked at her musingly. Almost as though he
had forgotten it was there, his hand remained at the
nape of her neck, entwined in the long, smooth strands
of her hair.

"How is your shoulder?" he asked at last. "I
thought I would come and see if you have finally

recovered from your accident."

"Oh, yes. Th-thank you. Sally mentioned only tonight that the bruises have all gone."

As if doubting the maid's judgment, he reached for the ribbon that closed the neck of her gown, and pushed aside the soft, white linen. His fingers flickered over the fading ridges of her scar, and Adrienne wondered if any woman had ever been known to die of suffocation, brought on by nothing more than proximity to her husband. She drew a deep breath and tried to pretend that she wasn't overwhelmed by an inexplicable longing to be enclosed within the protection of the Viscount's arms. She was paralysed with shock when his lips brushed lightly along the surface of her shoulder before he refastened the pale pink ribbons.

He did not say anything, nor did he make any move to leave the room, and the silence stretched out unbearably. He appeared absorbed in contemplation of the bed, which had already been turned back by the maid for Adrienne to enter. She jumped when he swung round suddenly and spoke to her again.

"Lady Abbott … Your mother … Did she tell you what marriage entails? Did she tell you what happens between men and women when they are married?"

She cleared her throat, hoping that it was too dark for the Viscount to see the blush that seemed to swamp her from the tip of her scalp to the soles of her feet. She cleared her throat again. "Do you think … That is, are you suggesting that you wish … that you think it is time … to provide Cravensleigh with an heir?"

In the candlelight his smile seemed oddly deprecating. "No," he said wryly. "At the moment I don't really care whether or not we give the estate an heir." With a sudden impatient exclamation he reached for her arm and pulled her roughly against his body. "Dammit, Adrienne, I don't find this the moment for talking about children. Let me *show* you what this is all about."

She opened her mouth to make some kind of protest, to say that kisses hadn't been included in her agreement to marry him, but it was too late. His lips had already pressed against her own and she discovered she had no desire to escape from the Viscount's arms. In fact, the movement of the Viscount's mouth against her lips was provoking such a powerful quiver of sensation throughout her body that she was forced to close her eyes and sway against him so that he could support her.

He gave a sigh of satisfaction. "You are very beautiful," he murmured against her lips.

"I can't stand up straight," she said, incoherent from the effect of all the strange feelings assailing her body.

He laughed softly. "That is easily taken care of." Before she had time to understand what he planned to do, he had gathered her up into his arms and carried her over to the bed. As she felt the cool linen of the pillows against her neck, a brief moment of rationality returned to Adrienne. "We cannot ... You don't love me ... You don't even desire an heir!"

"No," he said. "But I desire you – more than I had thought it possible to desire any woman."

"But ..."

"Hush!" He silenced her protests in the most effective manner possible, by covering her mouth with passionate kisses.

The candles had all guttered and gone out, long before either of them spoke again.

CHAPTER
TEN

Sally placed the tray of tea and buttered toast next to the bed and watched quietly as the Viscountess stirred in her sleep. It was unusual for her mistress to be fast asleep so late in the morning, and Sally peered at her with a touch of concern. Perhaps her ladyship was sickening for something?

Adrienne felt the silent scrutiny pierce the edge of her dreams. She turned reluctantly in the softness of the feather bed, her hand creeping out to touch the pillows, but she was quite alone. The creak of a wardrobe door warned her of the maid's presence in the bedroom and she pushed herself upright in the bed.

"Good morning, Sally." Her voice sounded husky and unfamiliar, as if it belonged to another woman. Perhaps it did. Surely *she* had not been the woman who exchanged those passionate kisses with the Viscount, and quivered in his arms with the sweetness of fulfilled desire.

"Good morning, my lady." Sally's prosaic voice returned Adrienne abruptly to the present. "It's a miserable old morning, my lady. Starting to rain. Pouring down, it is." The maid folded her hands politely and waited for her orders. If she saw that her mistress's nightdress lay in a ruffled heap at the foot of the bed, she was far too well trained to make any comment. Not a flicker of an eyelid revealed that she had noticed anything out of the usual routine.

Adrienne became conscious of the fact that she was naked beneath the covers and she hurriedly pulled the sheets higher around her neck. She was nowhere near as good at pretending blindness as the maid.

"I shall wear my new green sprigged muslin, Sally," she said, breaking the awkward silence.

The maid bobbed a deferential curtsy and turned to the wardrobe as Adrienne leaned back against the pillows, trying to pull her incoherent emotions into order. Her wayward thoughts refused to co-operate, however, and skittered repeatedly around the image of her husband.

As soon as she realised the direction her thoughts were taking, she gave an impatient shrug and forced herself to nibble at a corner of buttered toast. When the crumbs threatened to choke her, she got up and pulled on her dressing-wrap with brisk efficiency. This was just another ordinary day, she reminded herself.

She needed all her brisk reminders to force herself to concentrate on the maid's conversation. It was difficult to respond coherently when her thoughts had already taken wing. By the time she was dressed, Adrienne calculated that she had been awake slightly over an hour and had needed to remind herself fifty times to stop thinking about the Viscount. It was not a very auspicious start to a supposedly routine day.

There was no message from the Viscount waiting with one of the footmen when she came downstairs. She sighed, then chided herself for the fifty-first time since waking. She hesitated outside the heavy panelled door of the library, wondering if her husband was inside. She wished that she felt confident enough of her welcome to knock and enter boldly, as if she belonged by his side. She wanted to look at the Viscount's face and read the truth of his feelings in the depths of his eyes. Not even to herself could she admit that she needed to have the reassurance of feeling his arms once more around her.

A footman approached her as she hesitated outside the door.

"His lordship is with Mr Baggot, my lady. The bailiff requested an urgent meeting first thing this morning. Do you wish me to inform his lordship that you are here?"

"Oh, no!" she disclaimed, moving away from the library. "There is no need to disturb the Viscount." She felt absurdly shy, as if the change in her relationship with her husband must be branded upon her forehead, and she walked purposefully towards one of the garden doors, as if a tour of the garden headed her list of chosen activities for the day.

The rain had already stopped and since she was halfway into the garden, Adrienne decided to go and pick some roses. She collected shears and a straw basket from the head gardener, who insisted upon conducting her personally around the flowerbeds.

He was a dour companion, but despite his brooding presence Cravensleigh soon worked its usual magic upon Adrienne's mood. The scent of honeysuckle filled the air around her; the grass, freshly scythed, gleamed in a sheet of wet emerald brightness right up to the gates of the park. And always, at her back, the warm pink brick of the Manor waited to welcome her. Her feigned attention to the gardener's display of roses soon turned to genuine interest and she only returned to the house as the hour for luncheon approached.

She paused to accept the heavy basket of flowers

from the gardener at a small side entrance into the conservatory.

"Thank you," she said, dismissing him with a friendly smile. The gardens were so beautifully maintained that she forgave him his silence.

He gave a grunt, then bowed and broke into his longest speech of the morning. "Shall I send for a footman to carry the basket, my lady? 'Tis heavy they flowers be."

"No, thank you. The basket isn't too heavy for me to carry."

"Very good, my lady." The gardener gave another low bow before retreating to the hidden fastness of his potting-shed.

Adrienne smiled as she bent down to remove the thick wooden pattens she had tied on earlier. The gravel paths had been damp from the early morning rain, but her silk shoes were fortunately unstained. She pulled at the veiling of her hat, glad to shake her heavy hair free from confinement, and started to walk swiftly across the cool floor of the conservatory.

She was halted in her passage by the sound of her husband's voice, and a joyous light came into her eyes. His voice was coming through the ill-fitting door which connected one of the small family dining-rooms with the conservatory. An old friend must have come to call, she thought. She heard his voice again, even as her hand rested on the handle of the connecting door.

"But what is Marie-Rose doing in London?" asked the Viscount. "She told me she would be away for several weeks."

"Lord, James, don't expect me to interpret the female mind to you." Adrienne dimly recognised the voice of Arthur Travers. "You're supposed to be the expert, not I. She's *your* mistress, after all."

Adrienne froze into stillness, the words of happy greeting dying on her lips. Her hand dropped down from the iron latch of the connecting door. She could hear the frustration in the Viscount's words when he spoke again, and she wished that she had not become so adept at interpreting the subtle inflections of his voice.

"Damn it, Arthur, I don't want to take my wife to London. Not *now*. Not with Marie-Rose there."

"You don't have to bring the Viscountess. In fact, it's much better if you don't. That would really give the gossips something to prattle about. It will be easier to see the Comtesse discreetly if your wife isn't in town."

Adrienne could not bear to listen to their conversation any longer. The hot tears threatened to spill over on to her cheeks. She tried to swallow the sobs so that no noise would betray her presence in the conservatory. As soon as the tears were under control, she fled up the stairs to her rooms, indifferent to everything save the need to be alone.

She thrust herself inside her bedroom, slamming the heavy iron bolt into position before throwing herself on to the bed where she indulged in a storm of weeping. Clever! she thought with bitter self-derision. Lunatic, imbecilic, doltish, idiotic, would be better words to describe her behaviour. She must have been the world's biggest fool to believe that a notorious rakehell like the Viscount would fall in love with his own wife. Just because she had cherished his company during these past weeks, how could she have been naive enough to assume that the Viscount was sharing her feelings?

She was saved from an orgy of self-pity by the sudden blooming of a grain of anger. Pride came to her rescue where all other emotions seemed deadened by the impact of what she had heard. If the Viscount could dismiss her with two impatient sentences, she would certainly not oblige him by sitting at home and mooning over his departure. She tugged at the bellrope with an energy fuelled by rage. She poured cold water into the china washbowl in her dressing-room and splashed her eyes vigorously before going to her clothes press and flinging open the double doors.

"You rang, my lady?" Sally tapped at the bedroom door.

"Yes," said Adrienne curtly. She had no room left for smiles or pleasantries. "I want you to help me change quickly. It's almost lunchtime."

"Yes, my lady. Actually, my lady, a visitor is already waiting with his lordship in the small dining-salon." The Viscountess cast her maid a look of such blistering anger that Sally quickly changed her tactics. "That is to say, my lady, which dress were you wishing to wear?"

"This one."

Sally bit her lip, but she didn't venture any remark. If the Viscountess wanted to wear a dazzling new creation, designed for a formal London party, Sally was not about to make any protest. She laid out the dress and its shimmering underslip, as if her mistress were in the habit of changing her clothes three or four times a day. The Viscountess was already tugging at the buttons of the green sprigged muslin that had appeared to please her earlier in the day. From the scowl she was now directing at the mirror, it pleased her no longer.

Sally slipped the petticoat and the pink gauze overdress swiftly into place. She hooked the minute pink silk buttons with quick, nimble fingers. "Shall I brush the front of your hair, my lady?" she asked. It was the first breach in the silence of the room. "It's getting late, if you'd prefer to leave it."

Adrienne was already seated in front of the dressing-table mirror, ruthlessly pulling at pins and shaking her hair loose in a cascade of gleaming brown. "I want it like this," she said, looping some of the hair high on her head and allowing the remainder to fall in tantalising strands that swept across her nearly naked shoulders.

Sally gulped. "Yes, my lady." Her mind flashed back to the crumpled nightgown, and the indisputable fact that her mistress had been lying in bed this morning without a stitch of clothing. There seemed to have been a certain revolution in the Viscountess's attitude since the previous evening.

She combed her ladyship's hair with expert fingers, trying not to notice that the loops of hair, turned into ringlets by the curling iron, fell in positions that emphasised the fact that her ladyship's dress was cut shockingly low.

"There you are, my lady," the maid said finally. "Was that … Was that precisely the effect that you were wanting, my lady?"

"Yes." The Viscountess spoke shortly, without her usual smile. It might have been a magnificent stranger who stared back at Sally from the mirror. The pink and silver gown would have been daring as an evening dress, but worn during the day it hovered only just within the bounds of respectability. The Viscountess was always pale, but today her violet eyes blazed with a fire that illuminated her entire face. The bronze of her hair seemed to gleam with deliberate provocation against the white swell of her breasts. Sally swallowed yet another gulp.

"You look different, my lady."

The Viscountess smiled at last, but there was none of her usual warmth in the smile. "Yes," she said. "I have finally grown up, Sally." Abruptly she changed the conversation. "I shall see you after luncheon, Sally."

A footman opened the door of the small dining-salon as soon as he saw her walk downstairs, and Adrienne paused on the threshold so that the Viscount and Mr Travers could become aware of her entrance. The Viscount seemed to sense her presence and looked up. She could have sworn she saw a warm smile of welcome written on his features before it was replaced by a faint, puzzled frown. Nevertheless, his voice remained friendly when he greeted her.

"Adrienne, my dear, I'm glad that you were able to join us. When Arthur arrived unexpectedly, I tried to send one of the servants after you, but you seemed to have disappeared. You do remember Mr Travers, do you not? He is one of my oldest friends."

"Indeed yes. I knew Mr Travers before I even met you, my lord." She looked at Arthur Travers through seductively lowered lashes. "How good it is to see you again."

"And it is certainly a pleasure to be here, Lady Cravensleigh." The banality of his words failed to hide the gratifying effect she was having upon his male susceptibilities.

"Shall we sit down at the table?" asked the Viscount abruptly. "What have you been doing all morning, my dear? I was sorry that an urgent call from the bailiff prevented me spending some time with you before breakfast."

She was angry with him for pretending that he had regretted leaving her bed, so she treated Arthur

Travers to another languorous look from beneath her lashes. "Why, I have been busily fulfilling my domestic duties, my lord." She turned swiftly from Mr Travers back to the Viscount, so that the curls quivered against the upward thrust of her breasts. She felt a twist of perverse satisfaction when she saw that both men's eyes were transfixed by the sight of her trembling curls. "The gardener has been helping me to pick some roses." She allowed her limpid gaze to lock briefly with the Viscount's, before she spoke again to Mr Travers. "We are so pleased that you have driven all this way to see us, sir. But what prompted your visit?"

He seemed hypnotised by her eyes. "I have come about … That is to say, you probably know that your husband has an appointment from the King's court to the War Office. A minor problem has arisen in connection with the fulfilment of his official duties. In fact, Lady Cravensleigh, I have come as the bearer of bad news. I must request the Viscount's presence back in town."

She pouted prettily, as if the Viscount's departure were nothing more than a minor cloud on her blue horizon. "Oh la, Mr Travers, you need not feel guilty, I promise you. We have become as dull as toads here in the country. I dare say I shall be even more pleased to get back to town than my husband."

The Viscount thrust his empty wineglass in the direction of one of the footmen and spoke angrily. "It isn't convenient for you to accompany me. You will have to stay here."

Her violet eyes opened wide with feigned surprise. "Oh, I won't keep you from your official work, my lord. I just thought I would look at the shops, go to some parties, you know the sort of thing. It is positively an *age* since we did anything exciting."

"I thought you enjoyed the life here at Cravensleigh." The words appeared torn from the Viscount.

She managed to produce a hard trill of laughter. "Paying morning calls with the vicarage ladies and carrying food to your pensioners? La, my lord, you have a strange idea of entertainment."

The Viscount was white-faced. It was clear that he had forgotten all about Arthur Travers. "I had not realised that you viewed your time here in precisely that light. I thought you were different from other women." He paused to swallow some more wine. "Despite your feelings, madam, I must insist that you stay at Cravensleigh. It will not be possible for you to come with me to London."

Arthur Travers attempted to smooth stormy waters. "I don't suppose James will be away for long, my dear Lady Cravensleigh. He has a small matter of business to take care of, and then he will be free to come back and devote all his attention to you once again."

"Oh, I would not wish to keep him away from state business," she said. The Viscount looked up and she stared back at him fiercely, pride thrusting her head up high. "There is no reason for him to rush back on my account."

Arthur Travers stirred uneasily, hastening once again to smooth over an awkward pause. "Wonderfully understanding wife you have, James. I'm so glad I recommended her."

There was an immediate icy silence around the table. Arthur Travers coughed to cover his embarrassment and the Viscount flicked a finger towards the butler, who quickly ushered his footmen out of the room.

Adrienne just managed to contain herself until the door closed before turning to the Viscount. "I am delighted to hear that I came to you so well recommended," she said with dangerous calm. With heavy sarcasm, she added, "What did your obliging friend Mr Travers do? Draw up a list of eligible maidens so that you could take your pick?"

"Yes!" exclaimed Mr Travers, momentarily relieved to find Lady Cravensleigh so quick on the uptake. He caught sight of the Viscount's thunderous brow and hastily amended his reply. "Not a list, of course. Not at all the way it sounds. James was good enough to confide in me. Told me he wanted a wife and asked my opinion about..." Mr Travers floundered to a halt. He realised that his explanations, far from alleviating the situation, had simply made matters worse.

"I beg your pardon, Lady Cravensleigh," he said. "I am accounted a skilled diplomat, but I'm afraid I'm not much of a hand at making explanations to the ladies."

Adrienne smiled at him with frozen dignity. "Pray don't apologise, Mr Travers. I am flattered that I must have been placed so high on your list of selected ladies. Please do try some of our cook's blackcurrant tart. It is considered to be one of her specialities."

Mr Travers gratefully stretched out his hand and helped himself to a portion of the proffered tart and the Viscount pushed back his chair with a brief, angry exclamation. "Adrienne!" he said harshly.

"My lord?" She turned on him with a bright, blind smile that successfully masked the series of hurts she had suffered during the morning.

"You will have to excuse us for a minute, Arthur. We shall be back almost immediately," said the Viscount.

"Of course, of course. I quite understand if you have

something private to say to Lady Cravensleigh."
Arthur sprang to his feet as Adrienne got up from her
chair.

The Viscount walked into the adjoining
conservatory, gesturing to indicate that Adrienne
should follow. She thought wildly that it seemed to be
her day for dramatic revelations among the potted
palms.

"Adrienne," the Viscount said softly as soon as they
were alone. "It is not ... It wasn't as it sounds. Arthur
is a brilliant man, but he's a fool where women are
concerned."

"Is he? But then I am a fool where men are
concerned." She smiled tautly. "There is no reason
why you should apologise, my lord. We both knew all
along that this was merely a marriage of convenience
for both of us. Nothing is changed."

"Adrienne ... Last night ..."

She cut him off before he could tarnish the memory
of those few precious hours when everything between
them had seemed just right. "There is no need to
discuss last night," she said. "I am well aware of the
fact that the estate will one day need an heir. And I ...
and I am prepared to do my duty." Her words
stumbled over one another as she tried to think of the
sweetness of their lovemaking as nothing more than a
marital duty.

He caught her hesitation and misinterpreted the
cause. "I'm sorry that you found my attentions so
unpleasant," he said with icy formality. "Fortunately,
I shall be in London for the next two weeks, so you will
have some respite from your *duties*."

"When are you leaving?" The question was torn
from her reluctantly. It was not what she had meant to
say.

"As soon as we have finished luncheon. There seems no reason for me to stay."

"No," she said proudly. "I dare say I shall find plenty of ways to amuse myself once you are gone." She flicked one of the long ringlets away from the nape of her neck, conscious of the fact that the Viscount's eyes were still fixed upon her. "I won't come back to the lunch-table," she said. "I think I have more than fulfilled my wifely obligations over the past two days."

She turned to leave the conservatory before he could see how close to tears she had come, but her arm was seized and he pulled her roughly against his body.

"Not so fast, my dear Adrienne. It is also a wife's duty to bid her husband farewell." His lips were fiercely demanding as they closed harshly against her mouth, and yet she instinctively relaxed against him.

For a moment their kiss deepened then with a curt exclamation he thrust her away. "Don't overplay your wifely role, my dear. I might develop the mistaken impression that you actually enjoy it."

Adrienne stretched out her hand towards his retreating back. "My lord ..." she said softly. "James ..."

But the door had already slammed shut, and she was alone in the conservatory.

She looked miserably at the basket of brightly hued roses she had picked that morning. "Oh, botheration!" she whispered helplessly. "What on earth shall I do now? I wish Mama were here!"

The roses proved a poor substitute for Mama, since they had no answer to her question. Reluctantly, Adrienne retreated to her bedroom, where she could enjoy the solitary pleasure of worrying about the fact that the Viscount was every bit as callous and unfeeling as she had once suspected.

In the dining-salon Arthur Travers greeted his friend's return to the table with an apologetic frown. "Everything is all right with Lady Cravensleigh, I trust?"

"Oh, yes," said the Viscount. "Everything is splendid." Wearily, he pushed his hand through the thick disorder of his hair. "Why did Castlereagh have to choose this precise moment to tell the world that the Comtesse de la Ronde is a French spy? According to you, he has suspected her activities for the past year at least."

"Confidentially, James, the Prince of Wales met her at a party and was attracted to her. You know that he is between mistresses at the moment, and the Ministers all agreed that we couldn't risk Prinny falling in love with the Comtesse. He would be spilling state secrets into her sympathetic ears within hours of taking her to bed."

The Viscount shrugged. "Then arrest her. Lock her in the Tower, but leave me out of Castlereagh's troubles! I have no idea why he didn't order her out of the country when he first suspected her activities. Now he must face the consequences of his own decisions. I'm tired of picking up the pieces after our government staggers from one blunder to the next."

"The Comtesse has compromised a great many men in very high places. It would create a scandal of major proportions if Castlereagh had her arrested. The Minister simply took the easy way out of an unpleasant situation. He told the Prince point-blank what he suspected. Whatever his other feelings may be, Prinny is a loyal patriot and he drew back from his liaison with the Comtesse as if she had scalded him.

Of course, the spread of the rumours about her spying activities was inevitable once the Prince knew about it. Discretion is not one of his outstanding characteristics."

"But why do you need me, Arthur?" The Viscount toyed with his wineglass. "I might remind you that I am on my honeymoon."

"That is precisely why I posted down to you in such haste, my dear James, so that we can get this matter cleared up as quickly as possible. You know the Comtesse better than anybody else whom the Minister trusts. He needs your advice on how to deal with the situation and avoid a scandal that might touch Prinny. God knows, the Prince can't afford *another* scandal just at the moment."

"Does the Comtesse suspect nothing? Don't expect me to believe that she has no escape-route planned."

Arthur Travers sighed. "We had this conversation before lunch, James. I don't know why the Comtesse remains in London. She's your mistress, you tell me."

"She isn't my mistress any more," said the Viscount abruptly. "I am married now."

Arthur Travers could see no connection between the two states, but he was not prepared to argue the point. "Of course, of course, dear boy. Just as you say. Strictly between ourselves, old fellow, I believe Castlereagh may have prevented one of the Comtesse's attempts to escape and now, of course, he is regretting the fact that he didn't let her get away."

"So now I have to tear up to London and convince her to make a second attempt! I don't like it, Arthur. Not one bit."

"All the more reason to hurry to London and get it over with. Has your servant managed to get a valise packed, do you suppose?"

"Denby? Oh, yes, I am sure he will have everything ready. We can leave whenever you feel sufficiently rested."

"Then let us go right away. There is nothing to be gained by delay."

The Viscount pushed back his chair. "You are right," he said. "The sooner this matter is cleared up, the sooner I shall be able to return to Cravensleigh."

"Becoming a devotee of country living, James?" Arthur Travers laughed at his little joke.

"Yes," said the Viscount curtly. "Shall we go?"

CHAPTER
ELEVEN

Adrienne managed to fill the first three days after the Viscount's departure without too much difficulty. By dint of repaying calls on all those families who had left cards while she was sick, she was able to present a picture of busy preoccupation. She found time to check the cook's stillroom supplies and listened virtuously while the housekeeper discussed the state of the family linen. She even went so far as to visit the old barn beside the church which had once been used as a school and gave instructions for it to be cleaned and the walls freshly coated with whitewash, although the harvest was at least two weeks away. Fortunately there was nobody to see that she sobbed herself to sleep each night in a bed that seemed suddenly too large for one slender person.

On Thursday, four days after the Viscount's hasty departure, she woke up from a restless sleep, fired by a new determination to put her husband quite out of her mind. She would learn to enjoy the freedom of being her own mistress, queen of her little domestic empire. The determination lasted until lunchtime, when she realised that she was walking down the curved staircase mentally reviewing her négligés and wondering which one of them was most likely to compete favourably with similar items of clothing worn by a successful mistress.

With an impatient swirl of her muslin skirts, she

turned in the middle of the staircase and walked back up the stairs to her rooms. She tugged at the bellrope and waited for Sally to arrive.

"Yes, my lady?" Sally eyed her mistress nervously. The calm tenor of their days had been considerably disturbed since that memorable morning when she found the Viscountess lying naked in bed.

"I am going to London," Adrienne announced. "Please hurry up and pack some clothes. We need to get started as soon as possible if we are to reach London by Saturday."

"We … we are leaving for London this afternoon?" Sally repeated, incredulity colouring her voice.

The Viscountess was already halfway out of the door. "Yes," she replied. "It will take the grooms an hour to prepare the carriage, so *you* have an hour to prepare the luggage. I am going to inform the butler and the housekeeper that we're leaving."

Adrienne swept out of the door without a backward glance to see what effect her announcement had upon the maid. She was wise enough to know that, if she stopped to think about what she was doing, she would never leave Cravensleigh. The Viscount, after all, had been specific in his instructions. She could hardly justify her disobedience by telling him that she had left the country because she couldn't bear to spend another night alone in the bed she had once shared with him.

Her courage was at an even lower ebb by Saturday noontime when their travelling carriage finally drew up outside the shuttered windows of the Cravensleigh town-house. The doorknocker was muffled and there was no visible evidence that the Viscount was in residence. For a moment Adrienne's stomach lurched downwards towards her shoes. Her coach had taken two and a half days on the road. Was it possible that she had crossed with her husband travelling back in the opposite direction?

One of the postilions jumped down from the coach and banged on the black panels of the front door. Adrienne found that she was shivering with relief when she saw the butler, in full livery, appear at the entrance. After a brief, murmured conversation the postilion hurried back to Adrienne's carriage.

"The Viscount is still in London, my lady. He hasn't opened the house because he doesn't wish to publicise his presence in town. The butler says he can soon have your rooms ready to receive you."

Adrienne managed to disguise her heartfelt relief as she descended from the carriage. She greeted the butler with a smile and a polite inclination of the head. For once she was glad that Mama had spent so many hours teaching her how to conceal her true feelings. "I hope I am not putting you to a great deal of trouble," she said to the butler. "I decided to come and keep the Viscount company while he completes his business here in town."

"He will be delighted, I'm sure, my lady," said the butler suavely. "If you had sent us word that you were coming, he would no doubt have been here to greet you. As it is, I'm afraid he is away for the day and I shall have to ask you to wait for a while before we can serve you refreshments and provide you with hot water."

"There's no need to scold," she said with a little laugh, well aware of the reproof lurking behind the smooth words. "I know you're thoroughly put out that I didn't send one of the grooms on ahead with a message." She gave the butler a genuinely apologetic smile. "It was a spur-of-the-moment decision," she said.

The butler melted under the impact of her smile. "Your maid can make you comfortable while the servants prepare your rooms," he said.

"And the Viscount?"

"His lordship has been very busy, my lady. I am not sure precisely when he expects to return."

"It's not important. I dare say we shall meet up at some time or another." Adrienne did her best to sound casual, but apparently did not wholly succeed.

"His lordship is at the War Office, I believe, my lady."

Adrienne didn't think for a minute that he was at the War Office but could hardly say so. "Please send fresh ink up to my rooms," she said. "I wish to send a message to Lady Abbott, my mother. I hope we shall be able to see one another. I think she is still in town waiting for news of my sister's confinement."

"Very good, my lady. I shall send a footman with the ink immediately." He caught sight of one of the housemaids, scurrying through the servant's door. "Your rooms are ready, my lady. The shutters are opened and warming-pans have been placed in the bed if you care to sleep. Alphonse will have a luncheon available whenever you are ready to eat."

"Thank you," said Adrienne. "I am very grateful."

The hour for dinner came and went at Cravensleigh House, but there was still no sign of the Viscount. Adrienne paced restlessly around the drawing-room and finally put the chef out of his misery by agreeing to start eating dinner. There was no point in sitting and torturing herself any longer with mental pictures of the Viscount and the Comtesse de la Ronde dining at a candlelit table, set for two.

The butler escorted her solicitously to the massive dining-room table and cleared his throat once or twice as she sat down. "His lordship doesn't know you're here, my lady," he said. "There is no reason for him to send a message informing us of his plans."

"Of course not. I quite understand. Those buttered parsnips look excellent, please compliment Alphonse."

"Yes, my lady."

Adrienne struggled to swallow some food from the dazzling array of dishes Alphonse had provided for the first course. The excellence of the parsnips notwithstanding she didn't manage to make any very convincing inroads. The butler sighed and ordered the clearing of the plates with a curt signal to the waiting footmen.

Alphonse greeted the return of the untouched platters with an emotional outburst of Gallic disgruntlement, causing the butler to lose some of his calm. "Oh, give over, Alphonse, do. I 'aven't got the patience to listen to all that Frenchified gibble-gabble, not at the moment."

The butler supervised the serving of the second course with less than his usual allocation of dignity. He unbent so far as to attempt personally to persuade the Viscountess to partake of some of Alphonse's specialities. Adrienne obliged him by helping herself to a small serving of apricot cream and then pushing it around her silver bowl with her silver spoon until the butler thought he would scream.

To the relief of them all, she abandoned her desultory efforts to consume the wilting apricot pudding somewhere in the middle of her third spoonful.

"I have eaten enough," she said unceremoniously and got up from her chair almost before the footmen standing on either side of her were aware of what she was doing. She walked swiftly into the hall, unable to endure the sympathetic scrutiny of so many silent pairs of eyes. Another footman, bearing a crested letter on a silver salver, emerged from one of the service doors just as she reached the foot of the staircase.

"Oh, is that a note for me?" Adrienne approached him eagerly, hoping for a message from her mother.

The footman was young, one she hadn't seen before, and he blushed a hot scarlet. "N-no, my lady. This letter is for the Viscount. But there's a foreign maid in the kitchen, waiting for an answer."

"I will deal with it and tell you what to say." Coolly, Adrienne reached out for the letter.

The footman was new to his job, but even he knew that it wasn't a very good idea to let the Viscountess open a letter which had come from the household of That French Woman. The role of the Comtesse de la Ronde had been explained to him by a giggling scullery maid on the first morning of his employment.

"I thought the butler could deal with it, my lady," he said. "Not wanting to trouble you, like."

Adrienne raised a supercilious eyebrow, although inside she was shaking. "There is no need to take the matter to the butler," she said. "I have told you I will deal with it." She took the letter, her face still remote and haughty, but her stomach gave a sickening lurch as she broke the crimson seal. Her eyes scanned the contents. "Tell the maid who brought this that she can leave right away. The matter is being dealt with. What is your name?"

"Jim, my lady."

"Well, Jim, there is no need to mention to anybody that I have taken this letter. Please be sure that the foreign maid is told that the Viscount is away from the house."

"Yes, my lady."

"Thank you, Jim. That will be all."

She managed to walk with unimpaired dignity up the stairs to her room, but she was panting as she jerked open the bedroom door and threw the bolts into position behind her. She collapsed on to the bed and smoothed out the letter with shaking hands. The message was as unwelcome on the second reading as it had been on the first.

I learned today that you are still trying to persuade Castlereagh to order my arrest for treason. Come at once – tonight – or I shall inform your wife and the rest of the world that I am carrying your child.

The nausea which Adrienne felt was a fitting punishment, she decided, for opening the Viscount's personal correspondence. She pushed her fingers to her temples, trying to soothe away the pounding ache that had been growing ever since she first glimpsed the Comtesse's grim message.

It doesn't matter, she told herself repeatedly. Most men keep mistresses, so surely many men must discover that their mistress is with child? She had always known that the Viscount was having an affair with the Comtesse, so was anything altered because she had seen written proof of his connection? The child, in any case, must have been conceived before their marriage and probably even before she and the Viscount ever met. Adrienne gulped down several deep breaths and willed herself to be calm.

It was some time before these determined efforts were rewarded by a lessening of her nausea. As the sickness subsided, the significance of the other part of the note began to penetrate Adrienne's consciousness.

I learned today that you are still trying to persuade Castlereagh to order my arrest for treason.

A kaleidoscope of confusing thoughts swirled

through Adrienne's mind. Perhaps she had misunderstood the Viscount's reasons for rushing to London? Arthur Travers had claimed that he posted down to Cravensleigh on a matter of government business. Now that she gave the matter calmer thought, Adrienne realised that a busy man such as Mr Travers would never have journeyed all the way to Warwickshire simply to pass on some news about the progress of the Viscount's illicit love affairs. Even the butler had said that the Viscount was engaged at the War Office on a matter of business.

A tiny seed of hope began to grow in her heart. Perhaps the Viscount had wanted to be alone in London, not because he was madly in love with the Comtesse, but because he didn't want any scandal connected with his mistress's treasonable activities to rub off on his wife.

Adrienne read the Comtesse's letter for a third time. It was certainly not the effusion of a woman who basked in the knowledge of her lover's affections. It was, not to put too fine a point upon it, a letter threatening blackmail.

Adrienne's sickness was altogther gone, replaced by a burning desire to show her husband that she could be his helpmeet and not merely a decoration for his drawing-room. She realised just how much she wanted to share fully in the Viscount's life, his troubles as well as his moments of happiness. Even the thrill of becoming his lover and bearing his children would not be sufficient compensation if he closed her away from the day-to-day conduct of his life.

The thought of the Viscount's future children recalled Adrienne to the realities of the situation. She saw at once that there was a simple way to cut the ground from beneath the Comtesse's scheming feet. If she went to see the Comtesse and told her that she had read the note, the Comtesse would have no weapon with which to threaten the Viscount. Adrienne couldn't be outraged by hearing something she already knew.

But Adrienne wasn't sure she had the courage to face up to her husband's mistress and swallow the fact that this woman carried his child. She could visualise the Comtesse's beautiful features only too clearly and the fingers of jealousy closed round her heart, squeezing it into a tight knot of pain.

She forced herself to put the haunting image aside and took refuge in action. She pulled the braided bellcord and waited as calmly as she could for her maid to arrive.

"Send Jim, the new footman, upstairs," she said when Sally came into the bedroom. She didn't attempt to soften her command or to give even a partial explanation for her behaviour. Sally cared too much for her mistress by now and would spot an evasive explanation immediately. And the maid would be justifiably outraged if she knew what her mistress planned to do. It was better if she remained in ignorance, even if badly offended.

"Yes, my lady." Stiff-lipped, Sally bobbed a curtsy and went to summon the footman. Hurt was written all over her features.

Jim tapped anxiously at the Viscountess's door a few minutes later.

"Come in!"

He entered and found her ladyship clad in a simple daydress, a brown velvet cloak draped over her arm.

"I want you to take me downstairs and summon a hackney without anybody knowing I've gone out." Adrienne didn't ask him if he would be able to do such a thing. She was afraid of what he might answer.

Jim's complexion was alternately pale with fright and scarlet with embarrassment. He gulped. "There's servants all over the 'ouse, my lady. 'Ow am I supposed to get you out wivvout the butler seeing?" Awe-inspiring as he found her ladyship, there was little doubt in Jim's mind that the butler was an equally formidable personage to contend with.

The Viscountess tapped her foot in evident impatience. "I have no idea how you will do it, Jim," she said. "You have five minutes to decide which is the best route for us to take. Don't mention to anybody else where I have gone. At least for the next two hours."

"But where 'ave you gone, my lady?" asked Jim. "That is to say, where are you going, my lady?"

The Viscountess raised her supercilious eyebrow. Jim was beginning to dread that particular eyebrow. "I didn't know I was accountable to you for my movements," she said.

"Yes, my lady. I mean no, of course not, my lady." Jim bowed and hastened to the bedroom door, bowing again for good measure as he let himself out. In the corridor he mopped his brow. His fellow servants had all informed him that her ladyship was the kindest, most understanding mistress they'd ever heard tell of. Jim could only conclude that fourteen years as the son of a Camberwell pastrycook had not prepared him very well for kindness as practised by members of the aristocracy. He scurried to the back stairs and tried to decide how to smuggle her ladyship out of the house. Inside her bedroom, Adrienne resolved to apologise in person to the young footman before she returned to the country. The poor boy looked as though the events of the day had proved entirely too much for him.

In the end, Jim chose their escape-route well. The servants had retired to the kitchens to eat their own dinner. A solitary footman guarded the front hallway, and the back staircase was quite deserted as they crept down to street-level. Jim let the Viscountess out of an inconspicuous side-entrance and hurriedly escorted her out of the narrow mews, smelling of horse manure, into the main square.

"The hackney over there is waiting for you, my lady." The young footman still spoke in a whisper, wondering worriedly if he would be called upon to engage in many more nights of this nerve-racking intrigue. He thought longingly of Camberwell, and the pigs' trotters his mother used to boil for him as a Saturday-night treat.

Unexpectedly, the Viscountess smiled at him, a captivating smile that enveloped him in its warmth.

"Thank you, Jim, you have done well. You have helped me to do something difficult which I very much wanted to do.

Jim handed his mistress into the shabby hackney, bowled over at last by the charm the other servants had told him so much about.

"Wasn't nuffink," he said, then lowered his voice which had unfortunately broken on the final syllable. "Always 'appy to be of service to your ladyship."

The Viscountess smiled again. "Tell the driver I wish to go to Beekman Place," she said and turned away from the window, still smiling.

CHAPTER
TWELVE

Ever since Viscount Cravensleigh's marriage, the Comtesse de la Ronde had lived in a state of barely suppressed fury. Not only had she been foolish enough to betray her own deepest principles by falling in love with an English nobleman, but she had actually compounded her folly by loving one of the few men whose moral judgment remained untouched by her powers of seduction. She had realised over the past few weeks that she had never possessed more than the superficial attention of Viscount Cravensleigh, and she longed with a fervour bordering on madness to possess the whole, hidden soul of the only man whom she knew had eluded her.

The Viscount's marriage and his prolonged absence from London would have been painful enough to bear. But she was compelled to accept an additional indignity. From the gossip reaching her on all sides, the Comtesse deduced that the new Viscountess – the simpering, pallid English girl whom she had hated since first hearing her name – had succeeded in capturing the Viscount's heart where she, Marie-Rose, had signally failed.

Pain and anger combined to overcome her natural caution. Paid informers brought her hints that her run of luck in England was at an end. Her activities were

suspected in the highest circles of government and the
Comtesse knew in her heart of hearts that it was time
for her to make good her escape.

She knew that there would be a comfortable retreat
waiting for her in France. Contrary to the ill-informed
assertions of the British, who persisted in viewing him
as a monster, Napoleon Bonaparte honoured loyal
service and rewarded it well. The French government
would find a position for her somewhere in the Basses-
Pyrénées which had been her home. Despite her better
judgment, the Comtesse remained in England,
accepting the invitations of Society, hoping against
hope that the Viscount would return to town.

It amused her to captivate the ageing Prince of
Wales when she met him at a diplomatic reception
given by the Princess Esterhazy. She was gratified to
discover that her powers of attraction had not begun
to wane and her ruffled pride was soothed by the
knowledge that it required only one meeting to have
the First Gentleman of Europe whispering words of
seduction into her ears. But when the Prince dropped
her so quickly, despite his evident attraction, she could
no longer conceal from herself the real dangers of her
position. Her secret activities were obviously known.
Her arrest for treasonable spying might even be
imminent.

The Comtesse made hasty plans to leave the
country. Her love for the Viscount had not totally
blinded her to reality and she knew it was better to
leave for France and freedom than to dally in London
waiting for a lover who seemed unlikely to appear.
Having escaped the embrace of Madame Guillotine,
she had no desire to end her days on a British scaffold.

It was at this point that the Comtesse discovered she
had left her escape too late. The majority of her
servants and most of her informers, bound to her only

by money and not by ties of affection or patriotism, deserted her as soon as her troubles became apparent. Her former lovers no longer answered her notes. Gently, but irrevocably, Society closed its doors.

The Comtesse fought back mounting panic and bargained for a boat to carry her across the Channel. She fled to Dover, her jewels hidden in a false panel in her coach. At Dover, the smugglers' boat failed to turn up and she found the harbour-front mysteriously empty of other sailing-craft.

She tried to tell herself that it was merely chance; that the smugglers had been called out on a profitable job; that is was coincidence the harbour was so deserted. She could not believe her own reassurances. Her maid was frankly terrified.

All her previous concerns now seemed trivial, lost in a wave of fear. She returned to London, straining to maintain the elegant façade which was her trademark. Inside, she shivered with the remembered fears of a girlhood far too full of violent memories. Her supply of cash was low; her escape-routes seemed blocked. The Comtesse de la Ronde succumbed to terror.

It did not occur to her to turn to Viscount Cravensleigh for help. She knew that he didn't love her and she assumed that since she had no power to trick him into offering his assistance, there was no possibility he would be willing to help her as a friend. It was the last straw when she learned from her old maid, the only loyal servant she had, that Viscount Cravensleigh was in town and meeting with Castlereagh. She thought bitterly that, after months of sharing his bed (even if never his heart), she ought to have known better than to hope he would forgive her for spying against England. It never entered her head that the Viscount might be pleading her cause with the Minister and in a mood of mingled desolation and fear, she dashed off her threatening note.

Even in the depths of her despair, she was glad to seize upon a chance of wounding the Viscount. She knew, nobody better, how high the English nobleman held his honour and she wanted to hurt the Viscount as she had been hurt by his rejection. It was balm to her aching spirit to involve the Viscountess – the stupid English schoolgirl – in this squalid mess of failed intrigue and scandal.

When her maid returned from the Cravensleigh town-house it was still light, with the lingering pink glow of an English summer night. The Comtesse turned from her position by the window and spoke curtly.

"Well?"

The maid curtsied. After twenty years of shared exile, there was still no change in the formality of her relationship to the Comtesse.

"He is coming," she said slowly. "I don't know when."

The Comtesse concealed her eagerness. "You saw him?"

"No. But a footman told me that the Viscount would attend to the matter this evening. Right away."

"Help me to get ready. Tonight I must be at my most splendid."

"You, madame, whatever your temporary circumstances, could never be less than superb."

The Comtesse was moved by the sincere compliment, but she tossed her head impatiently. "*Ma foi*! I have been too long in this misty island. The fogs have entered my brain. I am beginning to listen to my own servants."

The maid said nothing, her face once more entirely blank.

"Come!" commanded the Comtesse. "Don't stand there looking like a nanny-goat chewing grass. We haven't much time."

Adrienne dismissed the hackney outside the door of the Comtesse de la Ronde's house. She noticed abstractedly that her fingers trembled when she handed across the silver coins to pay for her fare. She thrust the small pouch back inside the silk lining of her cape.

"Shall I wait, mistress?" The driver touched his whip to his hat. "They might not be 'ome, yer ladyship."

"Thank you. But there is no need for you to wait. I am expected." She walked up the entrance stairs quickly, before she could lose her courage and return to the fusty, safe interior of the hackney.

Her sharp rap with the heavy knocker had hardly died away before the door was opened. An elderly maidservant guarded the entrance and when she saw Adrienne, her smile of welcome faded.

"Yes, madame, may I help you?" she asked. The words were polite, but underlined with a faint note of antagonism.

"I would like to speak to the Comtesse de la Ronde."

"Her Excellency is expecting important visitors this evening. May I give her a message, madame?" It was clear that the maid was torn between two conflicting impressions of the caller standing on the steps. On the one hand, ladies of quality didn't go around late at night unattended. On the other hand, this caller bore the unmistakable stamp of inherited authority and delicate breeding.

"I should prefer not to stand on the steps," said

Adrienne. "Perhaps you would tell the Comtesse that Viscountess Cravensleigh is asking to see her."

A lifetime of training was insufficient to stop the maid's gasp. It was quickly suppressed. "Please to come in, my lady. I will tell the Comtesse you are here." Apart from the single gasp, the maid might have been an animated marble statue. She conducted Adrienne into a large, cool salon furnished with the stark simplicity of the French Directoire style. "I will fetch the Comtesse, my lady, if you will be seated."

She was not kept waiting long. She heard a rustle of silk in the doorway and she whirled round. Her heart sank as she confronted the Comtesse. Adrienne already knew her rival was a beautiful woman. Tonight, seen at close quarters, she was magnificent.

"You are asking to see me?" The Comtesse looked at Adrienne through brilliant glittering eyes. Her gaze travelled over the muslin gown, the dull brown of the velvet cloak and a faint smile twisted her lips.

"Yes." Adrienne forced herself to face up to the Comtesse. "I read the letter you sent to my husband. Viscount Cravensleigh will *never* submit to your threats. If you wish to tell the world you are carrying his child, that is your affair. I have a suspicion several other men could equally easily lay claim to paternity."

The Comtesse gave a small, hard, laugh. "But *I* shall say your husband is the father."

Adrienne lifted her chin proudly. "I don't suppose Society will listen to the rantings of a woman waiting trial for treason."

The Comtesse paled beneath her exquisitely-painted cheeks, but her voice remained strong, and scornful. "But what of you, my lady? How do you feel, knowing that your husband's child is going to be born in gaol?"

Adrienne looked down at her hands and saw they were shaking once again. She quickly pushed them out of sight.

"I find the thought almost intolerable," she said at last. "I can think of only one prospect which is worse, and that is that you should use me and your unborn child as instruments to blackmail my husband. I will not be used, Madame la Comtesse, and neither will the Viscount."

The Comtesse came suddenly to Adrienne's side and, with an insolent gesture, lifted her chin so that she could examine Adrienne's face more closely. "The Viscount doesn't have bad taste in wives," she said at last. "One sees why he has become infatuated with you."

Adrienne's eyes flashed with dark fire. "His taste in mistresses seems quite good as well," she said. "That is, as long as he doesn't expect honesty, or compassion, or loyalty."

For a moment she thought the Comtesse would strike her. "Why did you decide to come?" asked the Comtesse, no longer in absolute control of the anger in her voice. "Who knows you are here?"

"I have told you why I came," said Adrienne. "Your threats have failed, madame."

The Comtesse smiled. "Those threats were always empty, in any case. I am expecting nobody's child. Certainly not the Viscount's."

"But what of the note you wrote to my husband!"

The Comtesse shrugged. "I needed a weapon, that particular one came to mind. But you have been kind enough to provide me with a much better weapon, my dear Viscountess. To what lengths would the noble Viscount go, I wonder, in order to preserve *your* safety?"

"I am his wife," said Adrienne dully. She was so dazed by the Comtesse's revelation that her emotions were momentarily numbed. "Naturally, he feels an obligation to protect me."

The Comtesse laughed harshly. "The English miss has spoken! *Naturally he feels an obligation to protect me.*" She mimicked Adrienne's cool words. "*Mon Dieu!* You have shared his love and experienced his passion and you can talk so! You do not deserve such a man."

Adrienne turned away. "There is no reason for me to stand here and listen to your insults, madame." She spoke quietly, forcing herself to utter the words. "I am sure the Viscount ... that he will do his best to see your punishment is as lenient as it can be."

The Comtesse moved swiftly and slammed the doors of the salon, barring Adrienne's exit. "You do not think that I will permit you to walk out of here, taking with you my last chance for safety?" She smiled bitterly. "How easy it is to see, my dear Viscountess, that you have never before lived in danger of your life! What do you know about waking up each morning, wondering if this is the day when the mob will tear your house to the ground? What do you know about fleeing your home with only a few jewels stitched to your petticoat, scurrying for the cover of a peasant's cart every time you hear the march of soldiers' feet; hoping and praying that the scum who used to serve you will not now turn and slit your throat?" She halted the flood of words at last. "No," she said. "It is easy to see that you do not know the meaning of fear and panic. But you are going to learn, my lady, because I plan to keep you here until your husband agrees to arrange my escape to France. You have played into my hands, my lady. You have given me the ultimate weapon – yourself."

Adrienne tried not to let the terror she felt show in her voice. "You cannot possibly keep me here," she said. "It will be the first place my husband will look."

"Why?" asked the Comtesse. "Does he know that you are here?"

Adrienne started to speak and then fell silent.

"I am so glad that you did not attempt to lie," said the Comtesse. "I may be only the Viscount's mistress, but I know him well enough to realise that he would never have given you permission to come here."

"The Viscount was out when your note was delivered. But the servants know I have come to your house."

"Now you are lying," said the Comtesse. "I am confident that you took considerable pains to see that nobody knew where you were going." She saw the betraying blush creep into Adrienne's cheeks and she laughed. "You are a poor conspirator, Madam Viscountess. In France, during the Revolution, you would have been one of the first to pay obeisance to the cold steel of the guillotine. But I shall offer you the benefit of my own experience. Tonight I shall help you to learn how the threat of death can serve to sharpen the wits." She moved fractionally from her position at the centre of the doorway, and reached her hand towards the bellrope.

"Don't touch the bell," said Adrienne sharply.

The Comtesse turned her gaze round and her eyes widened first with disbelief and then with horror. Her hand fell away from the bell and back to her side.

Adrienne steadied the small, pearl-handled pistol in her right hand, pushing the folds of the brown cape back with her left hand.

"You are right, madame," she said coldly. "It is amazing what we find ourselves able to do in order to protect ourselves and the people we love."

"*Mon Dieu*! You surely do not expect me to believe that you can use that toy!"

"It is no toy," said Adrienne. "And I can assure you that I am able to use it. I shared my brother's lessons in marksmanship along with his lessons in Latin and Greek. My mother has always claimed that I was monstrously unsuited for pursuing the role of a lady." With steady hands, Adrienne moved a catch on the pistol. "The safety lock has now been removed, madame, so pray don't make me nervous by moving suddenly, or I cannot be responsible for my reactions. Please walk slowly towards the divan alongside the fire and be seated. I should, perhaps, warn you that this weapon has a hair-trigger."

Slowly, the Comtesse moved towards the seat Adrienne had indicated. "You will not get away from my house," she said. "The servants will stop you."

"I don't think so," said Adrienne. "A cocked gun is such an aid to persuasion, don't you think?" Carefully, keeping the gun aimed unwaveringly at the Comtesse, Adrienne backed towards the salon doors. With a steady hand, she reached behind her back and found the polished brass handle. "Goodbye, madame. Please don't follow me because I have no aversion to bloodshed and I don't wish to involve innocent servants in our quarrel."

Just for a moment the despair drawn on the Comtesse's features was replaced by a grudging respect. "Perhaps one day you will deserve the Viscount after all. At least you do not simper."

Adrienne gave a final twist to the door-handle, but as she did so there was a violent push and the door was flung open. With a superhuman effort, she managed to stretch her arm to one side, so that the pistol no longer pointed directly at the Comtesse's heart. The bullet, jarred out of the gun, exploded in a burst of acrid smoke.

Viscount Cravensleigh strode into the salon, tailed by the terrified French maid. His eyes swept round the room.

"Would somebody be good enough to tell me what the *devil* is going on here?" he asked.

CHAPTER
THIRTEEN

It was the elderly maid who recovered her voice first. Pointing an accusing finger at Adrienne, she emitted a scream of abuse. "She's the one! She came here to kill my mistress, that one. Ah, *sacré Dieu*! What have you done, stupid English girl, to my poor madame?" The maid tore away from the Viscount's grasp and rushed to the Comtesse's side, lapsing into a torrent of hysterical French as she tried to ascertain the extent of the damage which the gunshot had done.

"Enough!" said the Comtesse, pushing the maid impatiently away. She rose from her seat on the divan, holding one hand over the bloody wound in her shoulder. She spoke to the Viscount, ignoring both her maid and Adrienne.

"If you have come to arrest me," she said abruptly, "I would prefer it to be done immediately. I have already kept myself in suspense too long."

The Viscount held her gaze, ignoring the other people in the room just as she had done. "Why is my wife here?" he asked levelly.

The Comtesse hesitated for a moment before answering. "Your wife chose to come," she said and turned away to avoid meeting Adrienne's reproachful eyes. "I did not summon her. *Mon Dieu*, James! She is one person I do not need to see in my present circumstances."

The Viscount made no direct response. He turned towards Adrienne, who huddled close to the door, the pistol still smoking at her feet. He took her hands to pull her away from the doorway. His fingers were icy cold and there seemed to be no tenderness in his touch.

"Are you unharmed?" he asked finally. "Are you all right?"

She nodded. It was impossible to speak.

"Denby is waiting in the hall," he said without inflexion in his voice, his eyes blank as they swept repeatedly over her. "He will escort you to my carriage where you may rest safely. Please wait with him for me to join you. I must tend to the Comtesse's wound, and there are some other matters for me to arrange."

"It was not … I did not …" With a supreme effort, Adrienne cut off her attempt at justification. She did not want to make a halting explanation while the Comtesse stood, wounded and magnificent, in the centre of the Viscount's line of vision. She drew a shuddering breath and straightened, drawing herself to her full height. "What is going to happen to the Comtesse?" she asked.

The Viscount gave no indication of having heard her question. "Denby is waiting," he said. "I should be obliged, madam, if you would – just for once – do as you have been asked to do. Without argument."

She flushed at the rebuke and pulled her hands from his impersonal clasp. "As you command, my lord," she said and walked quickly through the door, cut to the quick that he seemed so indifferent to her state of turmoil.

Denby, in contrast to his master, greeted her with exuberant relief. "Thank God you're safe, my lady," he said as soon as he saw her emerge from the salon. "I thought *my* heart had stopped when I heard that pistol explode. We've been worried sick ever since we found out that you'd disappeared from Cravensleigh House."

Adrienne felt so dispirited that she scarcely listened to Denby's chatter. What did anything matter when it was clear that the Viscount didn't love her? "We are supposed to wait for the Viscount in his curricle," she said.

"Ah, and it's lucky there's still a whole carriage to wait in," said Denby as he escorted her from the house. "I thought his lordship was going to kill us both before we ever got here, and that's a fact."

"He was very angry," Adrienne agreed quietly.

"Angry!" Denby seemed surprised by her choice of word. "Well, he was certainly half-crazed with worry, my lady. Him knowing that the Comtesse was pretty desperate to escape and all." The groom broke off his explanations. "I'll just move over into the driving-seat, my lady. His lordship is coming out of the house right this minute."

Adrienne shrank back into the corner of the curricle. She wanted to throw herself into her husband's arms and weep against his shoulder, but she decided the Viscount was hardly likely to welcome such an emotional outburst, especially in front of his groom.

The Viscount climbed into the carriage and faced her across the narrow division of the interior. They might as well have been regarding one another across the Atlantic Ocean for all the warmth Adrienne could detect in his inspection. As soon as Denby had been given the order to depart, the Viscount spoke quietly to her.

"Would you be good enough to show me the note which the Comtesse sent to me. I assume you still have it?"

Adrienne drew the piece of paper out of the pocket in the lining of her cloak and handed it over to the Viscount. He read the brief message quickly and his expression, if it were possible, seemed to increase in remoteness. "At least Marie-Rose told me the truth of what happened," he murmured. He looked austerely at Adrienne. "Did she tell you that there was no truth in either of those allegations?" he asked. He stared out into the darkness of the London street. "I was not seeking to have her arrested," he said. "Neither was she expecting my child."

Adrienne swallowed hard. "The Comtesse admitted to me that her letter was a ruse."

The Viscount gave an angry exclamation. "Didn't it occur to you that these were the threats of a badly frightened woman? Did it not occur to you that there might be danger for you in going to her home? Have you no common sense at all?"

"Not very much," said Adrienne, stung by his apparent scorn. "I am only clever, but Mama has told me frequently that I have no common sense at all." If she had any sense, she thought miserably, she would never have fallen in love with such an unreasonable man. "Anyway," she added defiantly. "I took my pistol with me."

"Indeed you did! And nearly killed yourself!"

Adrienne's temper finally exploded. "No!" she shouted, forgetting Denby perched up on the driver's seat. "I did not nearly kill myself. I was retreating quite safely, with every problem taken care of, when *you* burst into the room and precipitated an accident." She swallowed hard, and thrust a fist against her mouth. She would not allow herself to cry in front of such an unfeeling husband.

The Viscount spoke harshly. "There is no need for you to remind me that I have handled this whole business wretchedly from the time I first met you. It is no thanks to me that you are not even now bleeding to death." He gave a self-derisory laugh. "And in the house of my former mistress, of all places!"

"How ... how is the Comtesse?" Adrienne asked. "Is she badly wounded?"

"It was a mere scratch," the Viscount replied. "The bullet grazed the flesh at the tip of her shoulder."

"I'm glad it is a minor injury."

For a few minutes they regarded one another in silence. Finally the Viscount moved so that he was sitting much closer to her in the swaying curricle. "Adrienne ..." he said tentatively. "Adrienne, I have explained all this so badly. Could you ... would it be possible for you to forgive me for allowing you to run yourself into such terrible danger?"

The curricle stopped with a sudden lurch that threw Adrienne against the Viscount. They both jumped back from the contact as if they had burned one another. Before either of them could speak, Denby had opened the curricle door, swung down the steps and waited for them to descend.

"Home again, my lord," he said cheerfully. "Everybody will be waiting to welcome you back, my lady. They *will* be pleased to see you!"

"Hell and damnation!" swore the Viscount beneath his breath as Adrienne led the way into the house.

The butler greeted them with a dignified smile. "It is gratifying to see that your ladyship is unharmed," he said. "His lordship, and all the servants, were very worried about you."

"Thank you," said Adrienne, but the Viscount

interrupted before she could say anything else. "We would like to be left alone for a while," he said. "Bring us some tea into the library."

The butler coughed discreetly. "If I might mention a visitor, my lord. Lady Abbott is in the drawing-room and has been waiting for some considerable time to see her daughter."

"My mother!" exclaimed Adrienne. "Oh, I shall be so glad to see her!" She rushed into the drawing-room.

"Hell and damnation!" the Viscount swore again, then realised he was repeating himself. "Are we never going to be alone?" he asked the butler.

The butler wisely decided not to answer this question, and the Viscount scowled before following his wife into the drawing-room.

He was greeted by the sight of his mother-in-law, comfortably ensconced on the sofa, sipping a glass of Madeira. He gritted his teeth in order to bite back yet another ungentlemanlike exclamation, and managed to kiss her fingertips with a fair imitation of his normal charm. "Lady Abbott," he said. "How delightful that you were able to call upon us *so soon* after Adrienne's arrival in town."

"Yes," said Lady Abbott with a happy smile, ignoring the none-too-subtle thrust. "I am leaving for Berkshire tomorrow and I couldn't believe the fortunate coincidence when I received Adrienne's note saying you were both in London. My dears! Such excellent news! Lydia has been safely delivered of twins: a son and a daughter." Just for a moment her features crumpled into an expression of faint astonishment. "Whoever would have thought it of Drexell? Two at once! And after only a year!" She quickly recalled the indelicacy of such frank speculation, for she clicked her teeth together and said hastily: "Do you have any messages for me to pass on to your sister?" She waited politely, trying not to notice the rigid set of the Viscount's jaw and the fact that Adrienne's attention seemed principally divided between unravelling the hem of her cloak and avoiding looking at her husband.

"The Viscount and I have no special news," Adrienne managed to sputter at last. "We have been leading very quiet lives, you know." She tried to give a nonchalant little laugh. "We have been buried in the country ever since the wedding, after all. Just give Lydia my fondest love."

"And pray add my congratulations," said the Viscount. "Would you excuse me for a minute, Lady Abbott? I must send a messenger to the War Office with some important information."

"Of course," said Lady Abbott as if she saw nothing strange in dispatching notes to one of the Ministers when it was close to midnight. "I shall stay with Adrienne until your note is written, my dear sir, and then I shall take myself off. I have to be ready to set out for Berkshire first thing in the morning. I can hardly wait to see my grandchildren!"

The Viscount bowed and murmured another graceful apology, before letting himself out of the room with a sigh of relief.

Adrienne followed his departure with longing eyes and then, with a visible wrench, pulled her attention back to her mother.

"You are looking very beautiful," said Lady Abbott. "Although I don't think much of your taste in evening gowns. Marriage must agree with you, child."

"Yes," said Adrienne and tore another few stitches from the hem of her cloak.

"Naturally, with the benefit of so many years of superior education, and with so much native intelligence, you are finding it quite easy to manage the Viscount. Even though, of course, he is what one might call a forceful man."

Adrienne shot her mother a look of mingled despair and chagrin. "You know very well that I am not managing the Viscount at all," she said. "Oh, Mama! Whatever am I to do?"

"Have you told him that you love him?" asked Lady Abbott.

"Well, no. Of course not," said Adrienne. "He ... he wouldn't want to hear such things from me."

"Why not? He chose you to be his wife. I imagine he would be gratified to hear that his feelings for you are reciprocated."

"But he didn't marry me because he loved me!" Adrienne cried out. "He married me to oblige his father." She blushed fiery red at having confessed so much. She immediately wished that she hadn't allowed the tensions of the evening to overcome her resolve to keep the facts about her loveless marriage hidden from the world.

"Poor Adrienne!" Lady Abbott stood up and brushed her hand affectionately over her daughter's gleaming hair. "So clever and so hopelessly lacking in feminine guile! I suppose the Almighty knows what he is doing. He has to protect the men of this world somehow, so he sees to it that the women who have brains never know how to use them!"

"You needn't think that the Viscount is overwhelmed by the power of my intellect," said Adrienne bitterly. "In fact, if you had heard him in the coach on the way back from the Comtesse's tonight ..." She blushed a shade of puce that reminded her mother of Mr Bagley's waistcoats and then fell hastily silent.

Lady Abbott looked at her daughter searchingly

and sighed. "I swear I never so much as *looked* at a book when I was carrying you, and I took particular pains never to think about anything that wasn't frivolous," she said. "I have no idea what addled your wits. It must be something on your father's side of the family." She gave her daughter another encouraging pat on the arm.

"I will refrain from asking what you were doing at that Frenchwoman's house," she said. "I'm afraid of hearing the answer. I shall just remind you that, out of all the women in London, the Viscount chose to marry you. For ten years he refused to marry to please his father, so I doubt if he married you just to satisfy some fresh whim of the Earl. No man is ever coerced into marriage totally against his will, my dear. Whatever rationalisations the Viscount may have given himself and you, he married you because he wanted to."

Adrienne looked up, her eyes alight with hope, wanting to believe her mother. She started to ask some question, but at that moment the Viscount came back into the drawing-room and she retreated once again into a shy silence.

Lady Abbott offered her hand to the Viscount in a gracious gesture of farewell. "It is excessively late," she said. "I will not detain either of you any longer." She cast one final exasperated look at her daughter and her son-in-law, who each seemed fully engaged in pretending that they were unaware of the other's existence.

Lady Abbott bent low to brush a farewell kiss against her daughter's cheek. "What's the matter with you?" she hissed. "Haven't you learned anything in two months of marriage? As soon as I've gone, cry, faint, tear your hair out, but make sure you end up by falling into his arms. And for heaven's sake, *don't think*.

Thinking is fatal, quite fatal, to the female constitution."

Adrienne sneaked a glance at the Viscount from beneath lowered lashes. He seemed to be ostentatiously engaged in de-tasseling the fringes of the satin curtains. "I can't help thinking," she hissed back to her mother.

"I know," said Lady Abbott sadly. "I blame myself." She swept towards the drawing-room doors. "Dear Viscount, pray don't bother showing me out. I think ... yes, I really do think, that poor Adrienne is feeling a little faint." She closed the doors firmly behind her.

The Viscount walked stiffly to Adrienne's side. "Is it true?" he asked hesitantly. "Do you feel faint?"

"I feel very strange," said Adrienne with perfect honesty. "Oh, James, please hold me. I don't believe ... I don't think I can stand up any more."

She swayed against him and he seized her into his arms, carrying her to the sofa and stretching her out upon the cushions.

"Adrienne! Oh, my God, Adrienne! What has happened to you? Speak to me!"

"Where am I?" she murmured obligingly.

"You are safe with me," he said. "I will always protect you from now on, my darling, however badly I have failed you in the past."

"What did you call me?" she asked, sitting up and opening her eyes very wide.

"I called you my darling," he said firmly. "And I must say that was a remarkably quick recovery."

She hastily sank back against the cushions. "I still feel dizzy," she said. She raised her eyelashes just long enough to give him a provocative glimpse of violet eyes. "I feel better when your arms are supporting me," she murmured faintly.

"Like this?" he asked, holding her close.

"Yes," she said, aware that her lips trembled beneath the intensity of his gaze. Slowly, deliberately, he bent his head to kiss her quivering mouth.

"Oh Adrienne, Adrienne," he said at last. "What am I going to do about you? How am I ever going to have a moment's peace, wondering what you're up to? My God, I thought my own life had ended when I pushed open that door and heard the gun go off."

"You certainly managed to hide your concern very effectively," said Adrienne.

He looked startled. "Couldn't you see that I was too shocked to behave rationally? Besides, the Comtesse was standing over the pair of us like an avenging angel. When I saw you huddled against the door and realised that it was *my* fault you were there, I hated myself so violently that I hardly dared to speak, for fear I would explode."

"I thought you were furious with me for wounding your … for wounding the Comtesse."

He trailed a pathway of kisses across her eyelids and then put his hand under her chin so that he could look deeply into her eyes.

"Before I met you," he said, "I found Marie-Rose an interesting woman. But I always knew that she was a cruel woman and an enemy of my country. She was my mistress, Adrienne, but I didn't love her. And once I had met you, she no longer even seemed interesting to me. I soon had no love left to give anyone but you."

"I didn't know you loved me," Adrienne whispered.

"I have loved you ever since you were knocked unconscious in the coach accident on our honeymoon," he said softly. "I thought for a few minutes that you were dead and I realised in those moments that I had really been waiting for weeks just for one thing: I wanted to have the pleasure of showing you Cravensleigh and making you my wife, the mistress of Cravensleigh in every sense of that word."

"I'm glad I didn't die," said Adrienne, slipping her arms around his neck. "I like being your wife, especially in every sense of the word."

For a long time there was silence in the drawing-room. The Viscount finally untwined his fingers from Adrienne's hair and started to pick up some of the jewelled pins that had been scattered over the floor.

"I think the servants have been sufficiently scandalised for one night," he said dryly. "We had better pick these up before I carry you upstairs to my bed."

"I can walk," she said breathlessly, although she wondered if that was altogether true. If the Viscount kissed her once more as he had just done, she wouldn't be able to sit upright, let alone mount a flight of stairs.

The Viscount flashed her a smile. "If you can walk," he said softly, "I must be losing my technique."

Adrienne blushed, and knelt down quickly to search for the last of her pins. "James, what will happen to the Comtesse?"

"She is being exiled to one of Canning's estates in Western Ireland," he said shortly. "She can do no harm there and if you had ever heard her hold forth upon the subject of British country life, you would know that she will find it a suitably severe punishment."

Adrienne looked down at her collection of hairpins. "I hope she gets back to France one day. I think she is very lonely."

The Viscount gathered her up in his arms and

walked determinedly towards the stairs. "I would not like it to be said that I am a prudish stickler for the conventions," he said. "However, I would like to point out that the very best of wives do not concern themselves with the fate of their husband's former mistresses."

"I will not interfere again," Adrienne promised. When the Viscount smiled at her in just that teasing fashion she would have promised to walk barefoot across a pathway of burning coals.

"You will not have the chance to break that promise," he replied. "I love you, Adrienne. There will never be another mistress."

"I'm glad," she said just as the Viscount reached his bedroom door.

"Why are you glad?" he asked as he set her down upon the silk cover of his bed.

"Because I love you," said Adrienne.

"That is good news," said the Viscount, pausing to bestow several kisses on his wife's shoulders. "Because we have a great deal of hard work ahead of us."

"My lord?"

"If you think I am willing to be upstaged by my brother-in-law, of all people, you are vastly mistaken. We shall have to produce triplets at the very least."

"I don't think, James, that triplets can be summoned up on demand. Even if one works very hard."

"You are possibly right," he said softly. "But I plan to have a great deal of fun trying. Kiss me, my love!"

The Viscountess Cravensleigh, mindful of her Mama's instructions, abandoned her attempt to correct the Viscount's misconceptions, and surrendered her lips to his kiss.